DARE THE SEA

DARE THE SEA

STORIES

ALI HOSSEINI

Curbstone Books
Northwestern University Press
Evanston, Illinois

Curbstone Books
Northwestern University Press
www.nupress.northwestern.edu

Printed in the United States of America

10   9   8   7   6   5   4   3   2   1

This is a work of fiction. Characters, places, and events are the product of the author's
imagination or are used fictitiously and do not represent actual people, places,
or events.

The book's epigraph is reprinted from *Marshlands* by André Gide, translated by
Damion Searls, published by New York Review Books, copyright © 2021.

Library of Congress Cataloging-in-Publication Data

Names: Hosseini, Ali, author.
Title: Dare the sea : stories / Ali Hosseini.
Description: Evanston, Illinois : Curbstone Books/Northwestern University Press,
    2023.
Identifiers: LCCN 2023021256 | ISBN 9780810146440 (paperback) | ISBN
    9780810146457 (ebook)
Subjects: LCSH: Iran—Social conditions—Fiction. | LCGFT: Fiction. | Short stories.
Classification: LCC PS3608.O823 D37 2023 | DDC 813.92—dc23/eng/20230509
LC record available at https://lccn.loc.gov/2023021256

For DW and Lee Miller

and for those who left
and those who stayed behind

Always and everywhere, we await
the revelation of things . . .

—ANDRÉ GIDE

CONTENTS

PART TWO

ACKNOWLEDGMENTS

I would like to thank DW, Richard Lindo, Lee Miller, and my agent Valerie Borchardt for their encouragement and suggestions and Randy Rosenthal for assistance in editing and many helpful suggestions.

The following stories were previously published: "Turning Bread to Stone" (as "Devil in the Bottle," *Guernica*, February 2012); "This Lame and Stubborn Mule" (as "Silence," *Story Quarterly* 46/47, Winter 2014); "When the Rain Stops" (as "Will This Rain Ever Stop?," *American Letters & Commentary*, November 2005); "Dare the Sea" (as "Sand and Shade," *Puerto del Sol* 40, February 2005); "Forty Degrees" (as "Earth Angels," *Epoch* 60, no. 2, May 2011); "Magic Island" (*Antioch Review*, Fall 2018); "Departures" (*The Coffin Factory*, November 2012); and "Day of Solitude" (*The Coffin Factory* 3, January 2012).

PART
ONE

CITY OF CHAOS

From the beginning of the year it was clear that something disheartening was taking shape in the small town of Sim-Aab. Something like an epidemic that slowly and mysteriously takes hold of the life of a community. During the winter, unlike other winters, the population was faced with a tremendous amount of rain, certainly very unusual for the arid climate. And then from the beginning of the spring, when the sun rose above the town, it seemed to stop there for an eternity and with one purpose only: to keep the town ablaze and boil the blood inside the heads of the citizens.

One hot afternoon, in the month of Khordad, Principal Roshan was busy preparing the sixth-grade diplomas. At the end of the month, he would hand them out to the graduating students and free himself from their noisy existence and the heat wave, and journey to the cool northern part of the country. The teachers were in the outer office, smoking cigarettes and engaged in serious debate. Principal Roshan was trying to catch as much of their conversation as he could.

The fourth-grade teacher, who seemed to have memorized what he was saying from a book, was speaking in a professorial tone. "No event is event-able, unless its event-ability is birth-able. Indeed, at the time when Event B is born from Event A, we can conclude

Sim-Aab – Silver Water.

3

that Event A must have had the hidden ability of Event B's birth and . . ."

"Well, my dear man," the third-grade teacher interrupted him, "in reality, you're repeating Aristotle's theory. He says the hidden ability that causes the birth of Event B must exist within the core of Event A."

At that instant, the piercing sound of the bell rang through the schoolyard. Principal Roshan turned toward the teachers, who were getting ready to go to their classes. "In simpler language," he said, "we can say that any event that happens is event-able."

A wide smile covered the face of the fourth-grade teacher. "Bravo, Mr. Principal," he said with a laugh. "You hit the nail on the head."

With the teachers gone, the office was quiet, except for the hum of the ceiling fan. After a few minutes, the shouting of the students from the classrooms died out. The principal went back to preparing the diplomas. The thought of the trip to the cool green part of the country was filling his head when the school janitor rushed in.

"Mr. Principal, please hurry, they've boiled over!" Then, turning on his heels, the janitor vanished with such speed that only his sarcastic smile was left hanging in the air.

The principal pushed the papers to the corner of the desk and reluctantly rose from his chair. God help us all, he thought, what's he up to this time? When he stepped out into the yard, he initially didn't see anything unusual. The teachers and students were in their classrooms. Like other days, the sun was aglow. But then, at the far end of the yard, he saw the janitor and a group of pupils in front of the latrines. The boys had their hands between their legs and were wiggling impatiently. When he got closer, a sharp odor burned his nose and he had to turn away.

The boys' elementary school was located a few streets away from the center of the town, with its ancient bazaar that attracted all sorts of people, its narrow streets and alleys clotted with cars and motorcycles, and of course its old mosque with the tall turquoise minarets that broadcast religious verses in all four geographical directions

4

from sunrise to sunset. The old town, thanks to the booming population of the last few years, was on its way to becoming a midsize city. Everywhere raw-brick and low-budget houses extended, without any sensible plan, into the wheat fields and lemon and orange groves at the outskirts of town. And this year, more than ever, the blazing sun started to bear down upon the town with swirling haze, dust, and swarms of flies. Through bad luck, this trouble, this misfortune, couldn't have chosen a better time and place, now that a mild chance of progress was on its way.

The school was the first place to fall victim to this scourge or ailment—in reality, Principal Roshan couldn't find the right word to capture the enormity of the disaster. After a few days, the same devil literally surged up from underground in different parts of town and in a short time caused a degree of disorder and confusion in everyday life that couldn't be described and was like nothing in the memory of the town.

The town, during its centuries-long existence, had tasted not only the sourness of defeat but also the sweetness of victory, and testimony to this were the ruins scattered nearby. The citizens were also aware of the sacrifices their town had made. They were proud of its standing up to the Greeks, enduring the Arab and Mongol occupations, and years later, blocking the attack of Agha Mohammad Khan coming over the narrow mountain pass from Afghanistan. Thanks be to God, there were people like Nader Shah Afshar, who freed the country from the invaders.

The history of the town goes on and on, but it would be better to stick to the present disaster that the town is challenged with. So, for now, those citizens whose patriotic feelings and pride in their past have risen, and who are eager to learn more about the history of their town, are referred to the excellent book *The Restlessness of a Restless People*, by Rashid Aldin Mohammad Ali Al'Rashidy. Bear in mind that no one has yet said a word about the type of malady the town is seized by at this time, possibly because they would have been ashamed to record such an unspeakable thing in any historical account.

The town, like any other town in this ancient country, or for that matter any town around the world where humans gather, is full of shopkeepers, shoemakers, office workers, carpet weavers, bazaari dealers, and vendors of all sorts and, it can proudly be said, people of many backgrounds and faiths—Muslims, Jews, Christians, Zoroastrians, and Baha'is—all free to practice their beliefs. And, like any other town, has its share of beggars, vagabonds, and unemployed, which has increased over the last few years, along with thieves and pickpockets, who gather around the main mosque and the teahouses and the small park. Everyone in the town was busy going about their affairs unaware of what was creeping right underfoot.

A few days before the school was caught up in the unfortunate situation, water was seeping up from the ground in the area surrounding the school. The dirty water around the latrines at the corner of the schoolyard invited swarms of flies and insects, an unbelievable orchestra of buzzing and hissing that wouldn't let the ears and minds of the students and teachers rest for a moment. The poor janitor—broom, mop, and pail in hand—was constantly busy mopping and cleaning.

The day before the disaster began, the janitor came to Principal Roshan, complaining that he needed to do something about the outhouses. "Sir," he said, "I don't know what the hell is the matter with this place. We just had the Tamizkaran brothers empty them a couple of months ago, and now they seem to be full again. Those rascals, those devil pupils, are always in there, doing devilish things—writing embarrassing notes on the walls, having urinating competitions, farting competitions." He puffed up his cheeks with air, and—purrrrrr—made a farting sound that embarrassed the principal, and then gave him a grin that showed his tobacco-stained teeth.

"My dear man," the principal said. "Is this something to joke about?"

"Joke, sir?" he grumbled. "Would I dare do such a thing? I'm certainly not making it up. These kids, these good-for-nothings, you should see what a mess they make. I have no hands or back from cleaning up after them."

Reluctantly, since there was a little money in the budget, Principal Roshan suggested that he go to the Tamizkaran brothers' shop and ask them to come and empty the outhouses. He left and the principal, having had enough of him, the heat, and the odor, had hardly finished a few of the diplomas when the janitor ran into the office again.

"Mr. Principal," he said excitedly, "the whole town is having the same problem. Everyone is looking for the Tamizkaran brothers. But they've vanished."

"What are you saying, vanished?" Principal Roshan asked.

"Disappeared, gone. Their shop hasn't been open for a week. Maybe they knew what was coming."

The principal couldn't listen anymore and his thoughts went to the students, not knowing what to do with a hundred and fifty nutty boys. Yet it was the janitor who came to the rescue. Every day he would gather the students together, a group at a time, and march them to the main mosque, in the main square of the town, where the public was allowed to use the toilets. He was very satisfied with this. First of all because it was his own idea, and second because it was an excuse for him to visit with the mosque's janitor. They would sit smoking their cigarettes, talking and laughing. They were the types that when it came to laughable things, would never come up short, especially with the disaster of the latrines and sewers spreading throughout the town.

Taking the pupils back and forth to the mosque toilets went on for a week until the janitor, wearing his sarcastic smile, ran into the office. "Mr. Principal, hurry up," he urged. "The mosque's toilets have exploded!"

"What do you mean exploded?"

"They've bubbled up," the janitor replied. "They're overrunning the place."

Suddenly the principal imagined all the students standing in a line in front of him, holding their hands between their legs and shifting in their places, trying to hold in their bladders. Turning to the janitor, he asked rather desperately, "What are we going to do now?"

7

The janitor shrugged his shoulders and lit a cigarette. "Don't worry, sir," he said. "There's always a way."

Not having more patience for the janitor and his way of smiling and twitching his eyes, Principal Roshan returned to his work under the creaking ceiling fan and visualized his journey north, leaving this place and everything that came with it. Sadly, he knew that his fantasy wouldn't have a chance to fly because with the recess bell the teachers would rush into the outer office and their everyday arguments and theories about the situation would commence. Would there be any practical suggestion or action that would help the state they were in? Of course not. Only talk, something they were undoubtedly very good at. "Well, what can we do?" someone would say. "Exactly," someone else would add, "it's out of our hands." "Right," another one would agree, "we need expertise." Someone else would disagree, and the words coming out of their mouths would mix with the smoke from their cigarettes and fill the small room.

It was after the incident with the mosque's toilets that the situation in the old part of the town took a turn for the worse. Everywhere, people were seen with water hoses, brooms, mops, and pails, washing and cleaning the yards, streets, and alleys—it was as if it had become a hobby for all. What had started in the back streets and alleys of the old town soon crept into other areas, where town janitors brought out the fire trucks and hosed down the streets, which in reality only worsened the situation.

Principal Roshan was surprised to see the janitor still taking groups of pupils in and out of the school.

"I thought the mosque toilets were out of business," he said. "Where do you take the students now?"

The janitor brought his head close to Mr. Roshan's ear and spoke with a fountain of smoke rushing out of his mouth. "Just between us," he said. "I take them to the public park."

Thinking he was taking them to help with the cleaning, the principal said, "That's not right—you shouldn't."

"Well, then," he said, "if you have a better solution, I'm at your disposal." And without waiting he went on. "Nothing to worry about, sir. I take them to the park, they go behind the trees, finish their business, and then I bring them back."

The principal again took refuge in his office and paperwork. Since, as far as he was aware, providing public toilets had never been a part of community order, and not just in their town, mind you, but in many others, it had always been the mosque's toilets that had done the job. Even with the mosque's toilets out of order, people young and old, especially those who came from the rural areas to shop in the bazaar and didn't know where to go, ended up there. And when the mosque's janitor had to chain-lock the out-of-order toilets, people had no choice but to head for the public park. At first, the authorities tried to stop it. Then they discouraged it. But when they themselves ran into the same problem, they had no other choice than to do the same.

Every day on the way to school, the principal's ears were filled with broadcasts pouring from the mosque's loudspeakers. "The misfortune that has come down upon our town is the result of blasphemy and unfaithfulness, the drinking and gambling that has been going on in this town. The Almighty will never forgive us, the way he didn't forgive the people of Sodom and Gomorrah, a people that were the epitome of everything he hated. So he struck them down by fire, turning their city to ash to be a lesson to us all. This is a test. The Almighty is testing us . . . We must get closer to God. We mustn't forget our daily prayer. We must go to the mosque every day. No Muslim should, at this unfortunate time, eat any melon or watermelon or tomatoes . . . the Imam's fatwa is that any fruit that causes the runs is forbidden until this affliction passes."

After the fatwa, the price of the forbidden fruits more than doubled. Trucks bringing fruit to town were stopped by the police. Grocery stores selling them were boarded up and the owners sent to jail. Of course, none of these actions worked, since a black market emerged right away, with yet more of a price increase. It must be mentioned that, adding to the ongoing chaos, the poor farmers, whose livelihoods had been based on their summer crops, had tons of melons and tomatoes on their hands that now went to rot in the fields.

The sun shone more mercilessly day after day. Flies and insects swarmed ever more happily. And confusion and anxiety took hold more thoroughly. Although the shopkeepers and other business owners helped the town-hall workers clean the streets every day and evening, the situation seemed to be getting not better but worse. Things at the school weren't any better either, and as usual the exchanges didn't advance beyond words.

"My dear fellows," the fourth-grade teacher would argue, "what we're faced with is that the fabric of our town is rotten. The town has been pregnant with this disaster for years."

"We need to abandon the city and go back to the fields and mountains," said the third-grade teacher. "The citizens of this city don't know the basic civilized way of life."

"Well, well, have some patience, my dears." The fifth-grade teacher, an older gentleman whom the principal had never seen get excited or talk much, put forward his view in a slow and deter-mined way. "Patience, my friends. We, the people of this town, will accept anything that unfolds upon us. We'll accept it and get used to it and live with it. Even worse than what we are facing, I prom-ise you."

Without the Tamizkaran brothers, people didn't know how to empty their latrines and the accumulating sewage. Every city and town had a few families like the Tamizkaran brothers, who for generations have done these sorts of jobs and due to the nature of their work lived on the outskirts of the towns, avoiding contact with others and others avoiding contact with them. They would be called "untouchables" in India, but in this area and this town they are known as "kannas"—cleaners. But in the last few years, the Tamizkaran brothers, whose name literally means "cleaners," had modernized. They didn't walk the streets and alleys, dirty and smelly, carrying tin pails hoisted on long poles, knocking on doors and calling out "Kannas, kannas!" They opened a shop in the main square of the town and did their job using pumps, hoses, and tanker trucks. And now they had suddenly, at the time they were most needed, disappeared. Their disappearance was the source of many rumors. There wasn't a day that the school janitor didn't bring some sort of news about them. Just the other day, he came to the principal all excited, saying that he'd found out the real story behind the disappearance. He went on to say that the Tamizkaran brothers, exactly a week before they went missing, had been emptying the well of an outhouse in the old town when they found something in the bottom. With much trouble, they managed to bring it up and wash it off, and see that it was a box made of stone. It was after this discovery that they and their families vanished.

Rumors of finding treasures around ancient ruins weren't something new, and the town was full of stories as old as the town itself. One was that the ruins on the outskirts of the town had been the palace of a prince, and that when invading armies came attacking the region, the prince, before running for his life, put all the palace's jewels in a stone box and dropped it to the bottom of a well, hoping that the enemies would be gone someday and he would return to his palace and rule of the region. If there was any truth to that, maybe the brothers had been lucky and struck gold.

A few days after getting the news from the janitor, the principal finished his end-of-the-school-year duties and went to say goodbye to his cousins, the Shahpourian brothers, at their place outside of town. He enjoyed being at the horse center and hearing about their efforts to breed the old race of Caspian horses. In the evening, they recited poetry from *The Epic of Kings* and discussed how the poet Ferdowsi so masterfully describes the horses and their riders in the heat of battle.

The next morning, he went back to school and handed the diplomas to the students waiting in the yard. None of them appeared happy. They looked tired and ill, with pale skin and wide eyes, giving him the notion they were suffering from some kind of disorder. All the teachers were gone, and he didn't see the janitor either. The school was filled with haze, dust, and the bad odor. Thoughts of the fresh, cool mountain air of the north country encouraged him to lock up the school as quickly as he could. Then he picked up his suitcase, which he had brought with him to school, and headed for the bus station.

As he got close to the main square, he could hear the mosque's loudspeaker more clearly. "For how long are we going to take it in this town? How long is it going to take for the mayor and those responsible for the well-being of our town to do something, to clean up and solve this problem? It doesn't matter how long, because as we know they are all corrupt and don't care about the people, only for their own pockets. It's time that we devoted Muslims come together, unite, and as the Imam said, clean the city of blasphemy. It's our religious duty. We need the Tamizkaran brothers to return from wherever they have gone. It's an order, and the good people of the town should go and look for them . . . We have no more patience . . ."

As the principal approached the square, he could see clouds of dust rising in the air and hear hammering and the sound of breaking glass. A group of men, women, and children, all in black, some carrying black and some green banners, were crossing the square on their way to the shrine of the Imam-zadeh in the outskirts of town to pray and beg for the town's safety. He made his way through the circle of people watching three men with picks and shovels who were attacking the Tamizkarans' shop. Dust covered the men from head to toe and made them look like identical triplets. One looked his way and then came toward him. The principal didn't recognize the school janitor under the whitish mask of dust until he parted his lips and gave him his sarcastic smile.

"What are you up to?" he asked the janitor. "Why are you destroying people's property?"

"Don't you see, sir?" The janitor pointed to the other two men. "With the help of the mosque and town-hall janitors, we're trying to open the shop."

"I see, but what for?"

"We need the pumps and hoses . . ."

"You're going to make trouble for yourself."

"Not at all, my dear principal, don't worry a bit." He brought his mouth closer to Principal Roshan's ear. "Let this be between us, sir.

We have support from the top. Haven't you heard the fatwa from the mosque's Imam? We should take control of the town. We have to put things in order."

"What things, what order?"

"The way our town runs," the janitor said. "It's all confusion and disorder. People go to the public park and do their business wherever they wish. The first thing that we are going to do is to divide the park into sections. Each class of people must have their own designated section. The bazaaris in one area, the town-hall people in another, the law-keepers in another. We ourselves, the educators, will have our own section as well. And there'll be a large area for the regular people and the outsiders who come to town . . ."

Principal Roshan couldn't say a word. He turned on his heels to get away from the crowd, the sound of shattering shop windows, and the sight of the janitor. But the janitor followed him and took his suitcase, saying, "Let me help you, sir. And don't worry a bit, my good man. I'll designate a nice part of the park for our school."

Like other days, the sun was shining sharply, and heat and haze rose from the wet asphalt. Groups of people, young and old, hurried in and out of the park. It was as if they had been used to this sort of coming and going for years.

At the Country Voyage bus station, the janitor put down the suitcase and wished Principal Roshan a pleasant trip and a good return. "You will be coming back, sir?" he asked. But without waiting for an answer, he turned to leave, in a hurry to get back to the distraction of the shop. He had gone only a few steps when he turned and looked at the principal for a long moment before calling out, "And Mr. Principal, who knows, God willing, I may find a treasure box in the bottom of an outhouse."

THERE'S A TALE
WITH THE WIND

On the slope of the hill, a group of men huddled at the edge of a hole. The round mouth of the hole opened to the sky and its collapsed walls funneled downward, as if sucked in by a devilish force from the heart of the earth. The men stood still, shifting their gaze between the hole and the two bodies they had pulled out and laid in the protection of the empty oil barrels. The wind, blowing hot and gusty, hissed through the piles of pipes and broken barrels and over the scattered pieces of bones and shards of pottery, then hurried on across the untilled fields, rounding up the loose tumbleweeds.

The young boy sitting away from the group couldn't take his eyes off Hesaam and Nezaam, the twins whose bodies were stretched out nearby. The sudden world of death—shocking and unexpected—had arrived in front of him.

The only sounds heard above the wind were a lone barking dog and the rumbling of an earth-digging machine at one of the brick kilns built on the neighboring fields in the last few years. A dump truck filled with bricks, dust rising behind it, lumbered along the dirt road leading to a town beyond the distant mountains.

"When will Hajji Habib be back?" a young man asked, standing up and shading his eyes to see the road better. "He's been gone a long time."

The boy turned to look, hoping to see the jeep that Hajji Habib had jumped into to go to town for a doctor. But he was certain that no one on earth could do anything now. He fixed his eyes on the water jar and the rope tied to its neck, coiled beside it like a snake. Just a short while ago, he had lowered the jar down into the trench to Hesaam and Nezaam. Then he'd offered water to the rest of the crew, who one by one put down their picks and shovels, wiped their brows, and drank eagerly. Afterward, he sat in the shade of the barrels, filled up the bowl for himself, and was about to take a drink when he felt the ground trembling under his feet and saw ripples on the surface of the water. A moment later, there was a loud tumbling sound and a fountain of dust burst into the air.

The men dropped their tools, shouting, "Allah help us!" They ran as if they'd seen a pack of wolves coming near their herds. Nothing was visible. Then through the settling dust they could see the collapsed wall of the trench, the deep circular hole, and the glint of a wristwatch on a hand extending out of the dirt, its fingers scratching the air and then growing still.

Everyone was stunned, not knowing what had happened or what to do, but soon they fastened a rope around Hajji Habib's waist and lowered him into the trench. Three other men followed. They dug furiously with their bare hands, flinging out the dirt until the heads and shoulders of the buried men were exposed. They hastily brushed off the men's faces and shouted for the water jar. Someone grabbed the jar from the boy and lowered it down fast. Hajji Habib tried to get them to drink, but the water leaked out of their mouths and ran down alongside their necks.

They'd forgotten all about the boy. It hadn't occurred to anyone to send him away. He stood at the rim of the hole and watched as Hajji Habib passed ropes under the arms and shoulders of the men and pulled them out. Their heads were bent down on their chests and their arms hung loose at their sides. The boy couldn't tell them apart, until he saw the missing leg and knew it was Nezaam. His thoughts went to his sister, Nilufar. What will happen to her now? he wondered. She was engaged to Nezaam and they'd been planning to marry after Nezaam had finished digging the trench for Hajji Habib's brick kiln.

But now Nezaam was dead, stretched out by the barrels beside his brother, his empty pant leg flapping in the wind. The boy thought back to Nowruz, the New Year, when the entire village had come to the hill for Sizdah bedar—the Persian spring picnic. The fields were green with winter wheat and the hillside was covered with buttercups and wild mint. Everyone was happy and enjoying themselves, not just because of the coming of spring, but also because of the engagement. They all participated in the games, the singing and dancing, and the footraces. Hesaam brought a pony from the horse stables where he worked for the children to ride. Nezaam won one of the footraces and told stories and made everyone laugh. Then came the revolution, the boy couldn't understand why or for what reason. The Iran-Iraq War broke out soon after and Nezaam, along with four other men from the village, was drafted and sent to the "jebheh"—the front—a new word added to the boy's vocabulary. Six months later, Nezaam came back with one leg but considering himself lucky.

"I told Hajji Habib not to build a brick kiln on this land," one of the older men said. He picked up a piece of brush stuck to his pants and the wind quickly took it from his hand. "This hill was a burial place in ancient times. But Hajji wouldn't listen. If his father, God rest his soul, were alive, he would never have allowed it. And now . . . look." He gestured toward the bodies. "We've lost two of our best young men." Then, as if noticing the boy for the first time, he called out to him. "My son, why are you sitting there? Get up. Get up and take yourself home . . . go back to the village. Today's job is done."

The boy didn't move. He sat staring, hoping that by some miracle the dead men would get up and resume their work as if they'd only been resting.

"My son," the old man pleaded. "Baba-joon, come on. Do us a favor. It's time for you to go home."

17

The boy was scared and wished he were somewhere far from there, far from the hill, the wind, and the dust that had been tormenting them since the day they started to dig. He turned toward the village. At the end of the fields, the low adobe houses of the village were barely visible in the haze. He didn't want to be the one to take back the news. How could he tell his sister? He knew that the instant he saw her, he would burst into tears. But he also knew that sooner or later, the news would reach the village, that maybe the wind would carry it, and the women, wailing, would come. And what would he do then? What could he tell Nilufar?

"May God Almighty help us all," said an older man with a short white beard, who was turning his prayer beads and speaking to no one in particular. "Hajji Habib started this brick kiln and now our two young men will never see the sun again." He shook his head. "Look at poor Nezaam. He went to the war and came back to find his death here."

"Brick kilns are popping up like mushrooms these days," said one of the younger men, pointing toward the coils of smoke rising from the neighboring kilns. "With all the destruction the war brought, there's more money in it than farming."

"God will punish those who start wars and cause suffering," said the man with the prayer beads. "And he won't forgive those who build brick kilns on fertile land and cook the priceless soil for bricks."

"Hajji Habib is a cautious person," another man said, taking off his hat and hitting it on the palm of his hand to get rid of the dust. "Before starting to build the kiln, he went to the mosque in town and asked the mullah to give his blessing."

"That has nothing to do with putting us down in a dangerous trench." It was a young man with a bushy mustache. "Hajji Habib will never recover from this disaster." He walked to where the boy was sitting, picked up the jar, and poured himself a bowl of water that he drank in one gulp. Then he ruffled the boy's hair and tried to give him a smile.

"It's all a test," said another man in low voice. "That's what I say. The Almighty is testing us. He sees the wrong things we do and lets us know about it in his own way. This old hill is full of spirits—it's a sacred place. Look at all the bones and the broken pottery we dug out. Maybe jinns live here and we shouldn't have disturbed them." He turned to the young man sitting next to him. "I was your age when foreigners came here from a faraway land they called Umrika and dug in the hills. They were here only three days when one of them fell ill. Before they had time to pack and leave, he died. What does that tell you? They desecrated the hills and were punished. And here we are. We shouldn't have desecrated this place either. Do you hear the wind?" He was silent for a moment, turning his face to the wind. "It's the hill moaning."

The boy listened, his eyes on the road. A dust devil wiggled by, spinning over the fields, gaining speed and gathering up the dust before rising high into the sky and heading toward the village. Then he saw something else, something whitish moving along the road. He stood up to see better.

"Here comes the doctor!" someone called out. The men stopped talking and stood up, straining to see. "What's the use now?" someone else said as they watched the car, a white shroud moving across the plain.

Soon a high-pitched sound, prolonged and piercing, rose to fill the heavens. The sound was new to the boy's ears. He wasn't sure where it was coming from, until he saw the white car speeding closer.

"See the women coming," someone said, pointing toward the village.

At first the boy couldn't see anything, but then he was able to make out dark patches, shadows moving in the haze. The women, all in black, cut across the fields and rushed toward the hill. For a moment they disappeared as they climbed in and out of a ditch that lay across their path.

The boy followed their progress and tried to spot his sister, but couldn't distinguish her among the dark figures. He had a feeling she was there though. The women hurried on, at times gathering close together and at times spreading apart, their chadors flying out like wings. Before long, he heard their cries rising and falling in the wind. Then he spotted his sister, running ahead of the others. She wasn't wearing a chador, only a scarf. His eyes started to burn as if there were needles wriggling in them. He hesitated for a moment and then flew down the hill. When he reached Nilufar, he grabbed her arm and tried to stop her, but she pulled away and ran ahead.

Everything seemed to quiet down. The car stopped at the bottom of the hill and the piercing sound ceased. Two men in white aprons got out of the car. In the silence of the hills, nothing was heard except the ululation of the women.

He didn't want to be there and ran down the hill toward the field. He knew that soon they would all come down. The men carrying the dead on their shoulders, followed by the women, all hurrying to the village cemetery to bury the bodies before the sun went down.

LAND OF MIRACLES

Marzieh Khanom entered the Radio and Television Building and started up the steps to the third floor. She leaned on her cane and stopped a few times to catch her breath. When she reached the Weekly Programs office, she pushed a few strands of white hair under her scarf and rearranged her black chador. The receptionist, who was in full hijab and seemed to be awaiting her arrival, showed her into the program director's office.

The program director rose from behind his desk and thanked her for agreeing to participate in the program, saying that her experience was a divine one and the devoted would be happy to hear it from her own mouth. Then he invited her to have a seat on the sofa by the window overlooking the square.

"We still have half an hour before the program starts. Would you like a cup of tea or a glass of water?"

She asked for water and then slowly sat down, holding onto the arm of the sofa. "It must have been something to see," she said, looking out the window that opened toward the busy square.

The director handed her a glass of water. "Excuse me?"

"The square, I mean. It must have been beautiful from up here." She spoke without taking her eyes off the fountain, now empty, its statue base askew and its pipes and nozzles twisted and broken. "What a shame. It was the most beautiful square in Shiraz. It was

21

famous for the Saa-at-e Gol—the flower clock. I wish I could have seen it from up here." She took a deep breath.

The program director went over to the window. Marzieh Khanom studied his face and graying beard and thought he looked like a man who had suddenly aged. He turned from the window. "Yes, it was beautiful. It was a different time—so many things have changed since then."

"Destroyed just because of the statue of the Shah," she said.

The program director walked over to his desk and stood there as if he hadn't anticipated the conversation. Then he came back and sat at the other end of the sofa.

"We were bystanders, really. The strikes hadn't reached us yet. All the problems had been at the religious centers and the universities." He looked out at the square. "I was at my desk and heard shouts of 'Marg bar Shah'—Death to the Shah. An angry crowd circled the fountain, trampling the flowers. They pulled out the hands of the clock."

"How could they do it?" the old woman said. "I'll never understand."

"It all happened so quickly," the director said. "Someone tied a rope around the Shah's neck and people chanted 'Allah-o Akbar' and pulled the whole thing down."

Marzieh Khanom turned from the square and the ruined fountain and looked at the director. "One of my neighbors was coming back from the bazaar and saw everything."

"It was the first major anti-regime act in our city," the director said, "and soon after came the burning of the cinemas and banks."

"Why so much destruction?" the old lady said. "Near the village where I'm from, there was a beautiful place with horses—it was attacked and burned down. The owners were good people." She sighed.

"You mean the Shahpourian place at Baaj-ga?"

She nodded.

"I knew it well. I made a television documentary about it. They were famous for their Caspian horses and training them as polo ponies. We didn't have anything like it. An exceptional place."

"Just like the fountain. I don't like any kind of destruction, my son," the old lady said after a moment. "If they wanted to bring down the statue, why did they have to destroy everything? The clock was the symbol of our town. And it's still a ruin after four years."

"There's a plan to rebuild the fountain and the clock." He reflected for a moment. "But we've heard that it will be a stone clock, with the names of the twelve Imams indicating the hours. And 'Allah-o Akbar' will be broadcast from a loudspeaker to mark the hours."

Marzieh Khanom was about to say something when there was a knock on the door and the receptionist said they were ready.

Marzieh Khanom walked into the studio alongside the program director, who showed her to a chair on the stage beside the announcer, a young man with a short beard who smiled and, half rising from his chair, welcomed her. In the middle of the stage was a table with a copy of the Koran and a vase of red tulips—the symbol of martyrdom. A huge poster of the sun rising from behind a cliff formed the backdrop.

She studied the cameras on tripods and the bright lights and watched the comings and goings of two men with headphones who were talking to the announcer. A few moments passed and then the announcer thanked her for coming and explained how the program would be conducted. She should just explain what had happened, calmly and simply, and everything would be fine. He pointed to the glass of water on the side table and said it was for her. She smiled and nodded.

At a sign from the program director, the program began. First there were verses from the Koran accompanied by drums and blaring trumpets. The cameraman moved closer and the announcer looked into the camera and started to speak. "In the name of Allah the most merciful, we welcome you to this week's program of *Land of Miracles*. Dear viewers, as you all are aware, every week we invite our brothers and sisters who have been privileged to receive the grace of Allah and experience a miracle to come to our studio and share their stories with you, the devoted. From the time that our dear Islam, with the help of our beloved Imam, received new life in our nation, we have been blessed. So blessed that not a week goes by without a miracle happening somewhere in our country."

Marzieh Khanom listened intently, without taking her eyes off the announcer.

"As you know, dear viewers," the announcer continued, "last week we had one of our young brothers, a soldier from the front, who was in the battle with the infidel Saddam and his military. He shared what he'd witnessed with his own eyes in the Holy War— our twelfth Imam on a white horse riding along the front, blessing our troops. Our twelfth Imam in absentia, whose final appearance we're waiting for, who with the help of Allah will come and cleanse this sinful world."

At another signal from the program director, the announcer stopped. The sounds of religious verses and trumpets and drums picked up again. The program director came to Marzieh Khanom and said that all she needed to do was to look at the camera and speak as if she were telling her story to him. She nodded and drank some water. A few minutes later, the reciting stopped and one of the cameramen pushed the camera closer to her.

"Dear viewers," the announcer said, "today we have a guest in the studio, one of the religious mothers of our town. She has received the kindness of Allah and has experienced a wonderful miracle. It's an honor for us to have her here to show us that Allah is with us and our country." He turned from the camera to face Marzieh Khanom. "And now, please tell us what happened last Friday, God's day."

The old woman rearranged her scarf, pushed her hair underneath, and shifted her gaze between the announcer and the cameraman.

"Please," the announcer said, "go ahead and tell us."

"Bessmelah o Rahman o Rahim . . ." She spoke in a slow, labored voice. "Yes, it was last Friday. I got up early as usual, said my morning prayer, and picked up my rationing ticket to get kerosene—my neighborhood's turn is every Friday. I took the empty bucket and walked to the nearby square. It isn't far, only two blocks away. There was already a long line, and the patrol was going up and down to keep order. Other weeks I would wait for hours and then get nothing or only a few drops, because there wasn't enough. But last Friday, I don't know how long I waited. I was very tired." She turned to the announcer. "I don't know if you've waited in line for things and how it is with all the people impatient and mothers with their children and all that—it makes you tired." The announcer nodded. "Anyway, I don't know how long I waited. I sat down on the ground waiting for the line to move."

She was silent for a moment, then moved her cane from one hand to the other. "I remember very clearly. You see, all those days I stayed in line, I was never mad at anyone, the people who cut in or things like that, but that day something happened and I pleaded to God. Dear God, I said, put fire to Saddam's house the way he put fire to our refineries, see how we have to stay in line for hours for a drop of kerosene. Then I said a prayer and asked God to give me strength and also for the war to end." She cleared her throat. "I don't know if I dozed off for a few seconds, I really don't remember, but when I stood up to move with the line and reached for my bucket you can't believe how surprised I was." She waited for a moment. "It was heavy and I didn't know what to think. A few people noticed. I unscrewed the lid and the smell of kerosene burned my nose. Then I heard someone shouting, 'A miracle—It's a miracle.'"

She stopped talking, a thoughtful look on her face, then turned to the announcer. "'What a blessing,' someone said. Someone else shouted, 'Allah-o Akbar—it's a miracle.' Everybody gathered round, looking at the bucket, smelling the kerosene and kissing my hands. 'Mobarak, mobarak'—congratulations, someone said. 'You're a special mother to have this happen.' They kissed the ground in front of me. More people were coming and I was getting dizzy with all the shouting and praying. If it hadn't been for my next-door neighbor who helped me get away, I would have been crushed by the crowd."

She grew quiet and leaned on her cane.

"Dear mother," the announcer said, "we're glad nothing happened to you. It must have been God's will that you not only experienced the miracle but were also saved from the crowd of good and devoted people who didn't mean you any harm. They only wanted to be blessed by touching your chador—the same way they go to the shrines of the martyrs to be blessed."

The old woman nodded. "Now, every day, people young and old come to my house to see me. They take my hand and kiss it. They don't need to do that," she said after a long pause. "I'm just an ordinary woman who raised a family. And now I'm old. I'm not special."

"Well," the announcer said, "you're special in the eyes of the good prophet Mohammad and all the Imams. That's why it was you who experienced the miracle and not any of the others in line. May Allah grant you a long life, dear mother. And thank you again for coming to our program and sharing your heavenly experience with our viewers." Then he turned toward the camera. "We've reached the end of our program, dear viewers. Goodbye until next week, when we'll bring you another story of a devoted person who has experienced a miracle."

The reciting of the Koran and the sound of drums and trumpets started up again. The program director came over and led the old lady out of the studio and into his office. He offered her a cup of tea.

She sat on the sofa and said that nothing could be better than tea at that moment. The program director thanked her and told her that she did a great job, that every word was sincere. She nodded and after a moment said that there was something that she had forgotten to say.

"Well," the director said, "that's understandable, given the situation. It happens to the best of us."

"I can't wait in line for kerosene anymore," she said. "People surround me and stare. It weighs on me. I can't walk to the corner store without being watched. I heard some people have even started to fight over the spot where I was standing. They say it's a special place, a divine place. I even heard that someone has started to charge people for putting their buckets there. What do you think of that, dear young man? People fighting over a spot on the asphalt?"

The program director didn't say anything, just smiled. And she, as if not in need of an answer, looked out the window. Darkness had descended over the square and she thought there was a group of people gathered around the ruined fountain. After she finished her tea, she got up, and with the program director holding her arm, they went down the stairs.

As soon as they were out of the building they found themselves in the midst of a crowd of people reaching out for her. "They've seen you on the show," the program director whispered, "and want to see you in person."

She leaned on his arm as they made their way through the crowd. She could hardly breathe and wished she were out of there and away from the crowd. The program director tried to hold them back, but the devotees were eager to touch her and kiss her hands and she was shoved in the rush of the crowd. A man reached out for her chador and tore off a piece, kissing it and rubbing it against his eyes as he murmured a prayer. More hands reached out, and her chador was torn off and ripped to pieces. "Allah-o Akbar!" "Salaam bar Imam Khomeini!" people cried out. The old lady was a small dark point in the crowd, her voice crying for help lost in the uproar of "A miracle, it's a miracle!" But the program director didn't let go of her arm and held her close, pushing the people aside until they made their way to the ruined fountain, where, by some miracle, a taxi waited with its door open.

RISING WATERS

Nana-Safar took Shamsi's hands and stared at her face. The thin layer of mud that she had rubbed over Shamsi's brow to ease her fever had dried, and her skin had taken on a pale color. Shamsi's eyes were closed and the circles under them quivered. Karamali led the donkey closer and asked Nana-Safar to hold the bridle. Then he lifted his wife and put her on the donkey's back. He took their infant from their teenage daughter, Golnaz, and held her up to Shamsi, who reached out and pulled the baby to her chest. The beads and magnets sown to the baby's wrappings to keep away the evil eye jingled and the donkey perked up its ears.

"Nana," Karamali said, "why are you so stubborn? Come on, go get your bundle. Let's get going before the sun leaves us. Can't you see that everyone's gone? They grabbed what they could and left days ago."

It was true. Everyone was gone. Zafar-Abad and all the surrounding villages were completely emptied out. Construction of the dam was in its last phase, and the villagers along the river had put the things they needed on their backs or loaded them on their donkeys or horse-drawn carts and left. The first to go were the "khosh neshins"—the merry ones, a term used by the locals to describe people who didn't own land and worked for others. They weren't as attached to the land as the rest of the villagers. For them, the building of the dam was an opportunity to be hired by the construction company. Next were the

29

small landowners, who had received some compensation from the Agriculture Department and moved to the nearby towns. But the peasants, who during the land reform a decade or so earlier—the so-called White Revolution—had been given a small parcel of land by the government, didn't have the heart to leave, knowing it would be the first step toward displacement and wandering. So they kept putting off leaving until the river rose higher and the government sent the gendarmes to drive away anyone remaining.

Nana-Safar and Karamali were among those who postponed leaving day after day, Karamali using his newborn baby girl as an excuse, and Nana-Safar in anticipation that her son Safar would be returning from his military duty any day. Nana-Safar, looking at the lines that she scratched on the wall of the house to keep track of the days, calculated that Safar was in his last month of compulsory duty. Karamali had tried many times to get Nana-Safar to leave, but she insisted she wouldn't take one step away from the village. "How could I?" she'd said each time. "My son will be coming home soon. Then we'll go together."

Shamsi gathered her strength and raised her head. "Nana-Safar," she said, drawing out each word, "farewell. And please forgive me for any pain or any discomfort I may have caused you. I may be on my last breath—who knows, maybe we won't have another chance to see each other . . . and will have to wait until Judgment Day."

Nana-Safar wiped her eyes with the wing of her scarf. "No, no," she said, "don't say that." She patted Shamsi's hand. "You've always been kind to me, like a sister. It's me who must ask for forgiveness."

"May God be with you all," she said to Karamali. "Go take your wife to the clinic. And don't worry about me—I'll be fine." Then she hugged Golnaz. "Don't cry, my girl. If I have any days left in life, God willing I'll put your hand in Safar's." She wiped the tears from Golnaz's cheeks with her bent fingers. "Take care of your mother. She has a fever. Make sure to stop and give her some water." She gestured toward the water jar loaded on the donkey. "My dear," she said to Shamsi, "don't disturb yourself, inshallah I'll see you soon."

Shamsi's head swayed back and forth with the movement of the donkey as they started out. "Let's get going, girl, the sun will be meeting the night soon," Karamali called out to his daughter, who was hugging and kissing Nana-Safar. "What am I to do?" he murmured. "The old woman has lost her mind and doesn't want to listen. Safar isn't a child that he would come here and get lost. If he comes back, he'll find us."

Nana-Safar stood on the mound by the village entrance and watched them leave, Karamali leading the donkey, followed by Golnaz. Each time Golnaz turned around to look back at her, Nana-Safar waved. She stayed until they disappeared from view and then came down and slowly walked home.

Nana-Safar was just past forty, but the sudden death of her husband years ago and having to work their parcel of land and take care of Safar had taken its toll on her. Her skin was wrinkled and her back curved. The bright thing in her life had always been her son Safar. He was engaged to Golnaz, and the plan was that as soon as he was done with his military duty and back home, they would get married. The marriage of her son was constantly on her mind, and she counted the days for his return.

At home, she put out some bread crumbs for her chickens and filled the broken clay pot with water for them to drink. Then she climbed the mud-brick stairs that led from the yard to the roof of the adobe house. She sat there, as she had done every afternoon for a week, pressing her knees to her chest and watching the road and the river that was rising higher every day. She sat until the sun was gone and darkness filled the empty alleys. No lanterns or fires flickered in the village night and the darkness seemed darker than ever. There was no baby crying or the sound of a lamb or goat seeking its mother. Her own rooster seemed uninterested in announcing the dawn—it was as if he knew that everyone had left the village. An owl from the ruins of a house called so mournfully that her heart sank.

The next morning, she got up early and walked among the deserted houses. Each house was as ruined as the next. The owners had pulled out doors, windows, and roof beams and taken

31

whatever they could. What a world, she thought, people destroying their own homes with their own hands. She passed by the piles of broken pottery, beat-up cans, and other unusable stuff that people had left behind. She decided to walk to the abandoned orchard. The orchard belonged to the landlord who lived in town and was watched over by his men until a few weeks ago, when people young and old rushed to pick the last remaining fruit. She searched among the broken trees for apples, apricots, or anything edible, dropping what little she found into a sack to carry home. Then she was startled by a rustling in the bushes and looked up to see the group of skinny dogs she'd seen roaming the empty alleys sniffing the piles of garbage. They were eyeing her. She waved her walking stick in the air, yelling, "Bereen gom shin, bereen gom shin"—get lost, get lost—until, to her surprise, they ran and vanished among the trees.

In the afternoon, she went to sit on the roof of the house. She thought she could see shadows moving in the old cemetery outside of the village wall and a shiver ran through her. Getting her courage up, she whispered to herself, "What's the matter with you, Nana-Safar? You've washed and put into the ground, by your own hand, ten, twenty, maybe more of the villagers and now the sight of the graveyard frightens you? Get ahold of yourself." She tried to push these thoughts away by thinking about her son, assuring herself that Safar would be back any day and they would go and find Karamali's family. Maybe Safar could find a job at the horse center at Baaj-ga, she thought. He was good with horses. She assured herself that Mr. Shahpourian, whom she had always heard good things about, would give him a job. Then Safar and Golnaz would get married.

As the days went by she found herself talking to her chickens. And, not being able to sit still, she wandered among the ruined houses, calling out to the families, as if they were somewhere inside and would come out. She couldn't understand how anyone could destroy their home with their own hand.

It became her habit to go to the cemetery every afternoon. "You poor ones," she would whisper as she walked among the graves.

"You're not safe either. I'm afraid you'll be washed away." She would visit her husband's grave and then her parents'. At dusk, she would light a lantern, telling herself that this way the dead wouldn't think the villagers had abandoned them. Then she would rush home, thinking Safar had returned. When she didn't find him, she would go up on the roof and watch the road, thinking about the day two military officers in a jeep took Safar for his mandatory military service, put him in uniform to send to a different part of the country, and gave her his clothes. She remembered how handsome her son looked in his new uniform. She hated to see him go, but was proud of him at the same time.

She tried to figure out when Safar would be back and how many days it was since Karamali's family left and she was alone. She counted the days, using her fingers and trying to remember what she'd done on particular days. She came up with six days, and counting again, seven. But she didn't give it any mind, thinking Safar would be back and they would find Karamali and the rest. Her last crumbs of bread were gone and she hadn't been able to find anything in the orchard, not even a rotten apple.

One evening she was sitting on the roof wondering what the dam was good for if their farmland was underwater. If their village was destroyed. And their animals were gone and people were displaced God knows where. Couldn't they have built the dam farther upriver? She heard a thundering noise coming from the river. She got up and looked in that direction, but couldn't tell what the noise was or where it was coming from. The sound subsided, and a moment later the sky in the direction of the dam brightened as if thousands of lanterns had been lit. She prayed silently and kept her eyes on the lights.

That night she couldn't sleep and noticed a damp smell, an odor in the breeze so bad she had to hold her scarf over her nose. She got up earlier than usual and went to the well at the far end of the yard and lowered the bucket. As she turned the old wooden wheel to bring up the bucket, she thought to herself that if by noontime Safar wasn't back, she would go to the river and follow it to the dam. "I'll go toward the lights that lit up the sky the other night.

There must be some people there. I'll sell my chickens, buy something to eat, and wait for Safar."

The wheel squeaked under her hands as she turned it. When the pail was at the rim of the well, she held the wheel with one hand and reached to grab the bucket, but the wheel slipped under her hand, turning noisily before the rope snapped and the bucket dropped into the darkness. It hit the bottom of the well with a splashing noise. Frightened, she sat down right at the mouth of the well and put her hand on her heart. It was beating like a tabla. She didn't move until the sunlight filled the yard.

That afternoon, Nana-Safar, a walking stick in one hand and a sack with her rooster and two hens in the other, hurried to reach the dam before the sun went behind the Zagros Mountains. The narrow dirt road stretched out along the river. It was rocky and made her tired, but she wasn't going to give up and stubbornly pushed on. After a while she reached a point where the road was totally underwater. The river was flowing calmly, but in her mind she saw and heard the roaring floodwaters of years gone by and remembered how angrily the river had come up to cover the farmlands and the roads and how she'd wrapped Safar, tied him on her back, and hurried up the mountain to escape the flood with the rest of the villagers.

Nana-Safar put the sack down and as soon as the chickens made some noise, hushed them. The river had grown tenfold but had a mysterious calmness about it. The muddy water was full of debris—brush, branches, plastic buckets, pieces of clothing, blankets, and other household items. She saw what she thought were bloated carcasses being pushed toward the bank, as if the river didn't want to carry them any farther. She wished she were somewhere else. She sat and took off her wet canvas shoes and put them in the bottom of the sack with the chickens and then struggled up the slope to get to higher ground. She had gone only a few steps when she suddenly slipped on the wet slope and tumbled down toward the river and was halfway in water. A fury arose from the chickens and her walking stick fell out of her hand and drifted away. Frightened and confused, she pulled herself up on her hands and knees, without letting go of the sack. Her clothes were wet, and her arms and legs were scratched and bruised. With shaking hands, she opened the sack and pulled out the wet rooster. Its head hung down to one side and its eyes were closed. She held up its head but when she let go, its purplish crown hung down loosely. The fear of death ran in Nana-Safar's veins and she thought she saw bloated carcasses, skulls with empty eyes and mouths bobbing up on the muddy surface. When she turned and looked up the slope, she saw a group of dogs, skinny and wet, watching her with narrow yellow eyes.

She was startled by the touch of a hand on her shoulder. A young man in a green uniform was bending down and looking at her. Frightened, she pulled away and looked at him for a moment. Then she threw her arms around his neck and kissed him on the cheeks. "My dear Safar," she said. "You're back. Ah, my dear son. I knew you wouldn't forget your mother."

The young man straightened up and looked at his companion standing beside him. Then he bent down again. "Dear lady," he said, "I'm not Safar. I work at the dam. Some people said you'd stayed behind in the village. You're lucky we found you, the water is rising fast."

But Nana-Safar wasn't paying attention to what he was saying. "My dear son," she said, "look how tall and handsome you've grown."

After being helped to the boat, she put her arms around the other young man and kissed him on both cheeks. "My dear Safar," she said, "I knew you'd come back."

The young man gave her water from a flask and then said he wasn't Safar either, but she appeared not to hear him.

"You came just in time, my dear son," she went on, "our farmland has been washed away. Our village is underwater. I don't know where everyone has gone. Look how the river's gone mad . . . It drowned my chickens . . ." She looked wistfully at the river.

35

"Karamali's family is gone too. Your fiancée left and we have to go and find them."

One of the men switched on the motor and guided the boat toward the lights of the dam. Then he turned to his companion. "Do you think she's from the same village as that family a few days ago? The man said an older lady was still at the village."

"What family? There have been a few of them."

"You remember, the man with the baby who had his dead wife on the donkey."

"Ah, yes," his companion answered over the cry of the motor. "He was the one who told us about the old woman." He shook his head and looked at Nana-Safar. Then he took some dates and an orange out of a plastic bag. He peeled the orange, wrapped the dates in a piece of nan, and held them out to Nana-Safar. "Dear lady," he said. "There's no need to worry anymore. You're safe now. You must be hungry, here's something for you to eat."

Nana-Safar let go of her grip on the side of the boat, took the bread and orange, and put them on her lap.

The man guiding the boat turned to his companion and said he thought the best thing would be to take her to Mr. Shahpourian at Baaj-ga. "Good idea," the other man agreed. "They've been very kind to folks over there."

Nana-Safar put a section of the orange in her mouth, then gripped the side of the boat again. "My dear Safar," she murmured, "I've been waiting for you. I've been waiting for this day . . . We'll go and find Golnaz . . . you will see how pretty she's grown. She'll be a good wife for you . . . We will find her and you will have the most fabulous wedding anyone has seen in our village."

36

TURNING BREAD
TO STONE

The pale-green barracks sat beside the asphalt road that curved
down the narrow mountain pass and stretched out across the desert. Nearby, on a low slope, was a white-domed berkeh ablaze in the
sun. In the desert where water is scarce, these domed structures are
built over dug-out holes to preserve rainwater running downslope
and keep it from evaporating in the heat. Some have quenched the
thirst of passing caravans for centuries and are considered sacred,
yet mysterious, by locals and the travelers who use them. This one,
almost ten meters in diameter with a huge dome above, belonged
to Buloor, a small village of low adobe houses the color of sand that
from a distance looked to be one with the desert and at times, as
the name suggested, shimmered like glass.

Inside the weather-beaten sentry booth at the checkpoint, a soldier leaned on his rifle. He was having trouble keeping his eyes
open in the heat until he was startled by the sudden rush of young
women and girls returning from the berkeh. They weren't chatter-
ing like other days and looked back as they hurried toward the
village. The soldier's sleepy eyes followed a woman's finger pointing
urgently back toward the berkeh.

In the few moments it took the confused soldier to run inside
the barracks and return with Corporal Asadi, the women and girls

37

had reached the date palms by the village and only the fleeting colors of their clothes were visible in the midday heat.

Zari was the first to see it. She stood under the narrow archway of the berkeh and stared at the shadow on the water until her eyes grew accustomed to the darkness and she saw her reflection and that of the domed structure. Water striders darted over the surface of the water, sending entangled webs of ripples toward the moss-covered walls. Zari could see the shadow only vaguely behind the narrow beam of light that extended down from a small hole in the dome and was filled with dancing dust particles. She thought it was a desert animal that had come in search of water and fallen in, but then she recognized a piece of clothing. Holding her breath and wondering whether the place might have become the house of jinns, she drew back and recited the name of God and the Prophet Mohammad. One or two of the other women stepped closer and glanced inside before they all rushed away, leaving their pots and jars behind.

Later in the afternoon, when the desert was giving off the day's heat and the air was pulsing with the raspy sounds of crickets in the low brown scrub, Corporal Asadi and a dozen soldiers stood at the berkeh, facing the silent villagers. A soldier pushed the tip of the barracks' flagpole into the puffed up sleeve floating above the water, carefully drew it toward the entrance, and with the help of another soldier, pulled the body out. The water running from the dead man's uniform sank into the soil, white with caliche, making a hissing sound. No one guessed that it was Sergeant Rozegar until the body was laid down on the ground. The villagers whispered and gathered together more closely. Corporal Asadi walked over to the body and bent above it. One side of the sergeant's face was smashed in and his eyes were open to the sky. His revolver was still in the leather holster on his hip.

Corporal Asadi stood up. Droplets of sweat glittered on his forehead. He stared at the dust-covered faces of the old men and women and the boys and girls. Then he waved them back and, cocking his head, spoke in a low voice to one of the soldiers, who turned and ran toward the barracks. The corporal gazed into the distance in a thoughtful manner before starting to check the area around the berkeh. With one knee bent to the ground, he examined the footprints and tire-marks of motorcycles imprinted on the soft soil. He took a pen and notepad from his breast pocket, scribbled something, and got up. Then he brushed the dirt off his knee and walked over to the villagers. Zari pushed the locks of her hennaed hair under her scarf and tried not to look directly at the corporal.

"When did you come here?" the corporal asked, stepping in front of her.

"At noon, sir," Zari answered in a low voice, her mouth dry.

"Were you alone?"

"No," she said, pointing to the women standing close by. "Hoori, Masomeh, the little daughter of Abbas, and—"

"Did you see anyone?"

"No."

"Then what are these boot prints and motorcycle tracks?" The corporal spoke angrily, pointing to the ground.

Zari gazed at the markings. "We didn't pay attention, sir." She was quiet for a moment and turned to look at the dead body. "As soon as we saw it in the water, we ran back."

"Where is Faraj?"

She wasn't expecting this question and was suddenly afraid for her husband, who should have returned from his trip by now.

"I asked about Faraj." The corporal raised his voice, his stained teeth showing.

Zari swallowed to moisten her throat. "He's gone to the Gulf to look for a job."

She knew that people like Corporal Asadi were familiar with this sort of answer. When women in the area villages were asked about their men, the answer was always the same, they'd gone to the Persian Gulf to work—when they were actually on their motorcycles going to the Afghan border or on their way back with packs of opium.

"I see," the corporal said. "Was he alone?"

"No, he went with Hydar, Abbas, and—"

"Did he go on his motorcycle?"

"Yes, sir," Zari said. The notion that the tire tracks could belong to Faraj's motorcycle worried her. How could the corporal tell if they were his? She didn't know if the tracks of motorcycles differed from one another and had never thought about anything like that before.

"Has he gone for a job or is he on his usual smuggling route?"

She looked away. This wasn't the same calm, smiling man who had been to their house. As he went on pressing her with questions, she felt weak in the stomach and thought that any moment she might faint and fall to the ground in front of the corporal and his soldiers.

She tried not to look at the dead body lying only a few steps away in front of the berkeh. Under her breath, she prayed to the Prophet Mohammad that Faraj had nothing to do with it. Maybe he had been here. He was due to return from his trip any time now. It seemed she heard the faint sound of a motorcycle last night.

Every time Faraj came back from the Afghan border he had to make another deal with Corporal Asadi. Depending on his mood, the corporal would sometimes be satisfied with coming for a home-cooked meal and at other times only with cash or a portion of the opium. When the corporal came to their house, Zari would have dinner and tea ready and would prepare charcoal for the opium pipe. Afterward she would go to Hoori's or Masomeh's house, only returning after she heard the corporal's jeep and knew he had left for the barracks. Then she would listen to Faraj complain that Corporal Asadi wasn't fair and every time asked for more. In the last three months, though, since the coming of Sergeant Rozegar, everything had changed.

The soldier came back from the barracks with a wooden ladder. He and another soldier picked up Sergeant Rozegar's body and put it on the ladder. They grabbed the ends of the ladder and started for the barracks, casting a long shadow that moved over the rough surface of the desert. The villagers followed them. The dead man's arms hanging down on either side of the ladder bounced with each step and drops of water from his sleeves pockmarked the dirt. At the barracks, they took the body in and the villagers continued on their way home.

Zari turned and looked back at the barracks. It seemed like only yesterday that Sergeant Rozegar had come to Buloor. At high noon the sergeant had stood in the village center and ordered everyone out of their houses. Barefoot boys and girls, old women in dark clothing, old men with their heads wrapped in muslin, and even the sick and infirm gathered in the village center. All except for the young men, some of them no doubt, the sergeant would guess, out on their smuggling route, and some hidden in the desert, not wanting to show their faces. Zari could still see the yellow dust flying out from under the sergeant's boots and the look in his eyes when he stopped in front of her and adjusted his glasses.

"I've come from headquarters," he shouted. "And if I find out that your village in any form or aspect is involved in opium trafficking, I'll strike you down in your own homes. I'll show no mercy even to your children or old people. Take the news to your husbands, your sons, your brothers." Marching up and down in front of the group, the sergeant had bragged about his bravery and how he had singlehandedly smashed the smugglers in other places, killing dozens and sending hundreds behind bars to be executed.

Zari trembled with each word and later swore to the other women that the sergeant's eyes were two different colors, one green and the other black. That same day a rumor traveled from mouth to mouth that the sergeant was a jinni who had taken human form, and by evening the old women of Buloor, carrying the Koran and murmuring prayers, were going slowly from house to house to expel the bad spirit from the village.

Corporal Asadi came to see Faraj a few days later, and Zari heard him saying that they needed to be careful and that Faraj should stop for a while. He assured Faraj that Sergeant Rozegar sooner or later would be gone. He said that in his many years of service, he'd seen other officers like the sergeant. At first, they showed toughness. But then, with the desert sun pounding down on their heads and the salty air cracking their lips, they eventually either gave in to the way things were in this part of the country or gave up and returned to their air-conditioned offices to sip lemonade and chat with other officers about their courage in breaking the smugglers' lines.

But soon Sergeant Rozegar proved to be of an altogether different sort. He neither accepted any payoffs nor let the sun and salt of the desert drive him away. By maintaining his grip on the checkpoints and keeping his soldiers patrolling the mountain passes day and night, he succeeded in arresting a few of the smugglers and confiscating their motorcycles, in this way limiting illegal activities in several villages in the area.

Faraj was frustrated at not being able to find a way to pass his merchandise through the checkpoint. One afternoon, when he was resting on the rooftop of his house, watching a group of women with jars and pots of water on their heads pass through the checkpoint on their way from the berkeh to the village, an idea came to him. That evening he told Zari about his plan and needing her participation. Zari shivered as he started to explain. "No, Faraj," she said finally, "I can't do it. I'm afraid of the soldiers."

"There's nothing to be afraid of," Faraj insisted. "You go through the checkpoint every day and aren't afraid."

"But I am afraid. You don't know how the soldiers stare at us when we pass. It terrifies me." She suddenly burst out, "Faraj, it's time to quit. It's a dangerous business and now you want to drag me into it."

"It will be only for a short time. I promise."

"You promised that after we got married you'd do this only for a short time to save some money and then we'd move to the city. Maybe it's a blessing that Sergeant Rozegar came here. It's a good time to leave Buloor."

"I haven't forgotten what I said. I've been trying but, you know, after what it costs to keep this old motorcycle running and bribe the officials, there's hardly anything left. If the sergeant hadn't come, we would have a chance."

He never saw her react so strongly. But in the end, he was able to convince her that with her help they would be able to save money because he wouldn't have to bribe anyone. He promised he would quit after a few more trips and then they would take their few belongings and go live in town.

After that, when Faraj received a parcel at the Afghan border, he would ride through the mountains and back roads, reaching the berkeh in three or four days. In the dark of night, he would pack the opium into empty Coca-Cola bottles, top them off with asphalt tar, and lower them to the bottom of the berkeh using a rope anchored under the surface of the water. The next day, Zari, going for water, would pull the rope up, put the bottles in her pot, and bring them home.

A long quiet night was passing in Buloor after a terrible day. Zari was lying on a blanket on the roof of the house, the scene of pulling out the body from the berkeh in front of her eyes. When she tried to fall asleep, two white eyes were watching her. She looked up at the star-studded sky, but the eyes were up there staring back at her. She sat up and listened for Faraj's motorcycle, but only the tense sound of crickets broke the silence of the desert.

Faraj's trips filled her with anxiety. If everything had gone smoothly, he would have been back by now. She was worried and prayed that the sergeant's death didn't have anything to do with Faraj.

She thought of the day she was coming back from the berkeh with the pot of water and the bottles and Corporal Asadi suddenly appeared in front of her at the checkpoint. She was so frightened that the pot rocked on her head and water splashed out and ran down her shoulders and chest.

"I know that Faraj is still at it," the corporal had said. "And he isn't paying his dues. Tell him I'll let it pass, but he should know that if Sergeant Rozegar finds out, he'll put a bullet through his head with no questions asked."

Trembling, Zari had hurried home and thrown the bottles down in front of Faraj. "There's a devil in these bottles. I won't do it anymore. I'm afraid they'll bring your death or mine. You're putting your life in a bottle, my life in a bottle, and when it breaks we'll be smoke in the air."

"Calm down, Zari," Faraj said.

"It's enough," Zari went on. "What was wrong with smuggling American cigarettes and blue jeans or Indian tea like you used to before we got married? Let's go away. Let's leave for the city right now."

"And what would I do there?"

"Maybe you could get a job at the sugar factory," she pleaded, even though she knew Faraj wasn't a man to take a job. "But I have another idea. Do you remember the woman we met when we took your mother to the hospital? She worked there washing the sheets and making the beds in the hospital. Maybe she could help me get a job at the hospital. If we stay here, for sure the sergeant or one of his soldiers will shoot you, and then what will I do?"

"For God's sake, Zari," Faraj said, raising his voice. "You think I don't think about these things? Or try to figure out what to do? We can't just go. We have to have some money. Do you think we can get it by selling the few kilos of dry dates we get from those old date palms?"

The nights Zari waited for Faraj she often thought about her mother, who never liked the opium trade or seeing the young men of Buloor become involved in it. She was always afraid of the barracks and its soldiers. "My dear Zari," she would say, "this smuggling never has a happy ending. Your father lost his life over a few packs of cigarettes he was bringing from the port, and my youth disappeared in a blink. What dark years. Who wished it upon us? I was pregnant with you, and your father would go away for months. In those days, no one smuggled opium and there were no motorcycles. They traveled to the Gulf by mule. I was waiting for your father the night the sound of gunshots came from the berkeh. How many were shot and who they were we didn't know. We had to wait until morning to find out. I'll never forget that night. It was like the sun decided never to rise."

Zari had heard the story many times, but listened quietly to her mother.

"The only man shot was your father. They shot his mule too. The men had stopped at the berkeh to drink, give water to their mules, and wash before coming home and were attacked by the gendarmes. It was by the mountain pass, where the barracks is now. The gendarmes came to the village the next day, and went house to house. Some of the young men had to go to the other side of the water—to Dubai and Qatar. They risked being drowned or captured by the coast guard, but they went. None of them returned except for Aabed. I think I've told you this, my dear Zari. Aabed was a nice-looking man. An old suitor of mine, but we never got married because our parents opposed it. After your father was killed, there was a rumor that Aabed had conspired with the gendarmes to harm him, but I never believed it. People like to make things up. Any of them could have been killed that night, even Aabed. Anyway, it was destiny. After Aabed came back from the other side of the water, he still wanted to marry me, but I didn't want to, not after your father died."

Zari had no memory of her father. But some years later, she had gotten to know Aabed, white-haired and half-blind from keeping his eyes open underwater when he worked as a diver for a pearl merchant in Qatar. She would see him sitting and telling tales of his adventures to the village boys in the shade of a date palm tree that was said to be the oldest palm in the village but had never born fruit.

Zari's eyelids were growing heavy when she heard footsteps and saw a shadow at the edge of the roof.

"Don't be scared. It's me."

It was her man—bony, tired, and dust covered. He lay down beside her. She pressed herself to him, thinking how long it had been since she had slept beside him. His traveling was always a source of anxiety, but this time had shaken her to her guts. She was tired of Buloor and its salty water and date palms rustling in the hot desert wind. She wanted to be in the city, to rent a room in a house with running water and a garden. She wanted to be in the crowded streets, to go to the bazaar and look in the shops full of goods shining under electric lights. She wanted to go to the cinema, the way they had done once when they were engaged. She wanted a big glass of ice water.

The warmth of the desert night was wearing off and their bare skin was absorbing the coolness of the passing breeze.

"Why were you late?" Zari asked, sitting up in bed. "I've been waiting and waiting."

Faraj was quiet.

"I can't help you anymore," Zari went on. "I can't go to the berkeh anymore. Let's go away right now. Let's leave before the sun comes up . . . you don't know what a day we had today."

Faraj was half-asleep, but sat up next to her. "I know," he said. "I saw everything."

"What do you mean?" Zari asked sharply.

"Calm down, woman. I was watching from the desert. I saw all of you at the berkeh."

"Did you go there last night? Maybe it was you. Maybe it was the tracks of your motorcycle that Corporal Asadi was looking at— Oh, God help us."

"What's with you, Zari? Calm down."

"Maybe you killed the officer. Allah help us. What are we going to do?"

"Me, a murderer? No, it wasn't me." Faraj was quiet for a moment. "I'm not a murderer. It was Corporal Asadi."

"What are you saying?" She stared at him. "Asadi killed the sergeant?"

"Yes, he did. Last night. I had just tied the bottles and lowered them into the water when I saw a car's headlights in the distance coming toward the berkeh. I jumped on my motorcycle and headed out into the desert. I thought for sure someone had found out about our hiding place. The car stopped at the berkeh and two people got out. They were shining their flashlights around, searching. After a while I heard a scuffle and voices. Corporal Asadi was talking angrily, saying, 'You think you can come here and turn our bread to stone.'

46

"Everything went quiet and the car sped away. I went to check the bottles and saw the body on top of the water. He was facedown, but from the uniform I could see it was the sergeant. I was scared and went back into the desert. I didn't know what to do. I wanted to go to the barracks but thought that they wouldn't believe me and Corporal Asadi would accuse me of killing the sergeant. That's why I didn't come home last night. I'm sure Asadi has already sent a report to headquarters and vowed to find the murderer. He could very easily prove I was there last night . . . I've been thinking about this all day. I think I have no choice except to go away for a while."

She listened, hugging her knees. He had told her everything and was starting to repeat himself.

"Dear Zari, there's no way out. I've got to go away. I'll go to the other side of the water. If that son of a bitch accuses me of murder, he'll send me to prison to be hanged, if he doesn't shoot me."

Zari wiped her burning cheeks. Her man had come home not to stay, but to say goodbye. She knew what it meant for a woman to have her man go to the other side of the water. In the minds of Buloor's women, there were too many of these departures. She knew she couldn't be like Hoori, who after so many years was still waiting for her man. Or Masomeh, married only six months earlier, who sat on the roof every day, watching the desert for her husband.

"What am I to do, Faraj? Tell me . . . You can't just leave me and go away."

"But I'll be dead if I stay—I know it. And what good would I be to you then?"

"I won't let you go. I'll come with you. I don't have the patience to wait and watch the road every day . . ."

Faraj took her hands in his. He kissed them and pulled her closer. She thought of their wedding night, how calmly and quietly he had held her hands, the only man who had ever touched her.

He kissed her. "My dear Zari. I wish I could put you on the back of the motorcycle right now and head out into the desert. But it's impossible. They may be out there waiting to shoot me—and you too. I promise, as soon as I go over the water and settle, I'll either come for you or find a way to have you come."

Dawn was spreading over Buloor. The sound of the motorcycle speeding away had died out long ago. Zari was sitting up in bed, holding her knees and rocking back and forth. Her temples throbbed and she felt ill. She stretched out on the bed and murmured a lullaby. Her mouth was dry and she stopped and sat up. The horizon was slowly lighting up, but the village was still asleep. She dressed and went downstairs to unearth the few coins that were in their hiding place in the corner of the room, money she had earned from selling last season's dates from their date palm trees. She picked up the small mirror and the wooden comb left to her by her mother, then folded her chador and the saffron-colored scarf Faraj had brought from Afghanistan on one of his trips. Finally, she took a string of dried dates, wrapped everything in a bundle, and put it under her arm. Without hesitating, she stepped into the alley, hoping no one would see her. She had never seen Buloor so pale and silent. She walked to the cemetery and found the tombs of her parents among the low dirt graves. The names of many of the dead and the way they had died were known to her since it was the habit of the villagers to visit the graves every Friday and listen to the elders talk about the departed ones. She sat between her parents' tombs, touching them and saying a prayer, then wiped her tears and got up. She didn't let her mind dwell on Faraj. For an instant she thought of going back to the village to say goodbye to Hoori and Masomeh, but was afraid their pleading might stop her from leaving.

Ahead, the whitish dome of the berkeh and the outline of the barracks were taking shape in the early morning light. Zari knew no women had left Buloor in this manner and that it wasn't usual for a young woman to travel alone. She was afraid—it was a new kind of fear—but assured herself that it would pass. She looked at silent Buloor and the vast desert that stretched south for many kilometers to the Persian Gulf. Then she squeezed the bundle under her arm and hurried toward the asphalt road that snaked through the mountains on its way to the city.

BLACK MOUNTAIN PASS

"Hey, Tohamtan—get up, boy. Are you still asleep?"

It's Uncle Sadegh calling from the roof of the house next door. The boy opens his eyes. The stars are still flickering in the sky. The air feels cool and light. The boy turns over in the warm bed.

"Hey, Tohamtan. The sun will be up soon. We need to get going." As long as the boy can remember, his uncle has called him Tohamtan, after the legendary warrior from the *Shahnameh—The Epic of Kings*.

He stares into the dark. It's quiet but he can hear the wind starting to blow. He thinks it will be a hot day. They need to start early and reach the quarry soon after sunrise and make it back up Black Mountain Pass before the day turns hot, otherwise the radiator will boil over. But it seems that no matter the time of day, the engine gets too hot and steam rushes from under the hood. Then Uncle Sadegh boils over as well. "You dumb piece of crap," he says, "must you always do this to me? It's no time to break down now, you good-for-nothing."

Before his uncle calls out again and wakes the neighbors sleeping out on the roofs, the boy gets out of bed and goes down the wobbly wooden ladder. He picks up the bundle of bread, cheese, and dates that his mother has left for him and walks to the dump truck parked outside the village gate. He checks the oil, pours a bucket of water into the leaky radiator, washes the windshield, and starts

49

the engine. A few minutes after it roars, his uncle appears, his gray hair disheveled and his eyes sleepy. He climbs behind the steering wheel, recites the prayer "Van ya-cad-o la-zine kof-ra-ho" seven times, asking God to keep them safe and away from the evil eye, and they start off.

The old Leyland truck is everything to Uncle Sadegh. When he gets behind the wheel, it's like he has the world in his hands. Two years ago, his uncle convinced the boy's mother to sell the small farm that was their inheritance, promising he would make some money so they could move to Shiraz for the sake of the boy and his future. He quit his job working for Hajji Habib, took the money from the sale of the land, and disappeared. Day and night the boy's mother watched the road and prayed for his return. "My poor brother," she would say. "He's not a match for those city businessmen and they'll get the money out of him." A month later, a faded brown truck pulled up to the gate and Uncle Sadegh jumped down from behind the wheel in front of the astonished villagers.

Tohamtan started helping his uncle after finishing sixth grade, the last grade at the village school. Fall and winter they haul sugar beets from area farms to the sugar factory in the nearby town, and spring and summer carry stone from the quarry and bricks from the kilns into town and to the surrounding villages. Sometimes they take barrels of molasses from the sugar factory or a load of oats to the horse center down the Baaj-ga valley. Many times in the middle of the night, they've driven to the town clinic with a woman about to give birth or someone ill or injured on a job or in a fight. On these occasions Uncle Sadegh won't take money, saying that people don't have much and they have to help out when there is need. And always, on the day of martyrdom, they take people to the shrine of the Imam-zadeh Sultan.

They pass the graveyard and the area where the villagers have dug out dirt to make mud bricks for building houses. The boy remembers the rainy day his uncle and the tractor tumbled down the hole. He had been working for Hajji Habib, who owns much of the land in the village, and was returning from plowing a field. All the village ran out to see the tractor upside-down at the bottom, its huge tires spinning in the air and splashing up the falling rain. His mother's cries of "God have mercy!" flew across the graveyard. After digging for an hour, the village men got to Uncle Sadegh and pulled him out from under the tractor. Wet and covered with mud, he looked around, his eyes wide. It seemed he didn't know what had happened or where he was. Then he sat on a gravestone and lit a cigarette. He was okay, except for the small cut on his brow that left a scar.

The sun is up by the time they reach the main asphalt road and stop at the checkpoint. Like other days, Uncle Sadegh has a bill ready for the police. The bribe that lets him drive without a license. And soon after, they are at the mountain pass, where the shrine of the Imam-zadeh, with its green dome and black banner, sits amid the boulders close to the road. Beside it is a slim stream and a lone tree with thorns and small leaves. His uncle says it's a konaar tree. The branches are tied with strips of cloth, some green and some black, put there by devotees pleading with the Imam-zadeh to grant their prayers and cure the sick or put a curse on those they dislike. His uncle nods toward the Imam-zadeh, murmurs "Aslam-o-alikom," and gives the boy a coin. "Go drop it in the charity box." Then he prays for their safety and the truck and they head down the mountain pass to the quarry.

The boy is happy when they finally, after the many twisting curves, are through the pass and reach the plain. His uncle asks him to open the dashboard and hand him the recorder. It's often the case when they're on the flat road and nothing has gone wrong with the truck. He watches as his uncle puts his elbows inside the steering wheel, brings the recorder to his lips, and starts to play. "Don't be afraid, kid," he says, when he sees that the boy is nervous. "It's your uncle Sadegh driving—he's an excellent driver." The boy thinks of his mother, who always prays they won't have an accident on the road and will return home safely.

They get to the quarry just before noon and eat their lunch while they wait for the truck to be loaded. The boy is relieved it's not a blast day. He hates having to hide behind a huge boulder and cover his ears. And if he says something, his uncle smiles and says, "Be brave, boy, be brave. You aren't named after a hero for nothing." It surprises him how a mountain can be blown up, that a mountain, so enormous and tall, can go to pieces. What power dynamite has, he thinks, that it can crack the mountain and take it down like that. At the quarry, he's seen the sacks with the words "Dangerous – Handle with Care" written on them in big red letters. Once he asked his uncle how dynamite was made. "I don't know," his uncle said. "Maybe it's like gunpowder and is made of different chemicals and powders. All sorts of things come from the mountains, you know. God has put many things under the mountains, and we humans keep finding them, but we waste lots of them."

By the time the truck is loaded, the sun is high and the day has turned hot. They drive out of the quarry and reach the main road. A few kilometers away, in the foothills of the mountain, they pass the horse center with its big iron gate and stone wall encircling a grove of sycamore and willow trees. Last summer they took a load of oats and horse feed there. The boy thinks of the huge house and wide porch shaded by trees. Mr. Shahpourian, the owner, offered them lemonade and melon and asked his name and whether he went to school, then told him he could pat the ponies tied to a tree by the porch.

It's one of those days when the heat shimmers above the asphalt. The truck, heavy with its load of stones, roars and smokes as it goes up the mountain past the dark cliffs that flank the pass. Uncle Sadegh keeps one eye on the road and one eye on the radiator gauge, and they're almost at the top when steam shoots out from under the hood. He gives the truck more gas, not wanting to stop on the dangerous part of the road. "Come on, you worthless piece of shit," he says. "Take us up there . . . *cooome onnnnnn*."

When they make it to the top, he pulls off to the side by the Imam-zadeh and tells the boy to hurry and get the pail that hangs on the side of the chassis. Uncle Sadegh opens the hood and the boy fills the pail from the stream running by the Imam-zadeh and hands it to him. He splashes water against the engine. It's something they do often to cool the engine down. But the steam hisses and keeps coming with no sign of slowing, until the motor goes *put-put-put* and shuts off.

When the steam clears, the boy carefully twists off the radiator cap using a piece of cloth and pours in a pail of water. His uncle climbs behind the steering wheel and turns the switch, but the engine clicks without turning. He tries a few more times and then comes down and plays with the engine for a while, but can't make it start. Then he gives up and says he's going to town to get Mohammad the Mechanic.

The boy sits under the tree where its branches throw dancing shadows over the ground. A hissing sound vibrates up from the arid surroundings. He feels for his uncle since something always goes wrong with the old truck. He thinks of the evenings the villagers gather around his uncle, his hands black with oil and grease, trying to fix the truck. And how they nudge one another, saying how the dealers in Shiraz cheated him and sold him a no-good truck. Your name is Sadegh, they say, the "honest one," but were they honest with you? And then they laugh. They boy wishes his uncle would tell them to shut up and stop harassing him, but his uncle doesn't say anything and keeps on with what he's doing. He's heard his uncle telling himself he would be happy if he could leave and never see these people again.

The boy doesn't like looking at the shrine. Inside, it's dark and smells of burnt candles. The tomb is covered with a dusty green cloth. And there are praying beads and sheets with prayers scattered around. He wishes the truck had broken down by the horse center and he was sitting on the porch drinking lemonade. He hopes his uncle got a ride and will soon be back with the mechanic. He tries hard to keep his eyelids from closing and then hears the sound of whimpering.

Three women dressed in black come out of the shrine. They tie pieces of green cloth to the tree and pray, their eyes closed and their lips moving silently. Then they sit by the stream, wash their hands and faces, and open a small bundle of bread and dates. The women give him a friendly smile and offer him some bread and dates. "Eat, my son," the older woman says. "You look hungry." When they get up to leave, he watches them, three dark shadows walking toward the bright sun.

Then he hears a truck changing gears as it comes roaring up the pass. He doesn't remember eating, but sees date pits by his feet. He washes his face in the stream and drinks some water. The shadow of the tree is stretched out long in front of him, and he thinks he's been waiting for a couple of hours. More time goes by before a jeep pulls up to the truck and his uncle and Mohammad the Mechanic get out. Mohammad the Mechanic tells his uncle to turn the switch and listens to the engine. There's only a low *click-click*. He works on the engine for half an hour, smoking cigarette after cigarette. Then he turns to Uncle Sadegh. "You said you splashed water on it, right?"

His uncle nods.

Mohammad the Mechanic lights another cigarette and looks at Uncle Sadegh and then at the boy, giving him the feeling he's being studied. "Sadegh Khan," he says, "you've done it again, man. Another masterpiece. What's in your head, man? What did you think, splashing cold water against an engine burning like a furnace? You've not just jammed the engine, you've cracked the cylinder head as well."

It seems his uncle doesn't understand at first. He turns away from the mechanic and looks at the silent truck and then at the Imam-zadeh.

After Mohammad the Mechanic gets into his jeep and drives away, Uncle Sadegh kicks the truck and curses, then picks up a stone and throws it at the Imam-zadeh. "Is this what I deserve?" he says. "After all the offerings I threw into your donation box?" Then he sits down under the tree and lights a cigarette. The boy anticipates more cursing, but his uncle is drawing interlacing lines on the sand with a twig and doesn't say anything. The boy can see the scar on his forehead. Once in a while he looks up at the truck and the Imam-zadeh.

"What are we going to do now, Uncle?" the boy asks.

"I don't know," he says, "I'm tired of all of this. It's not worth it. The little money we make goes into the police officers' pockets as a bribe, or we drop it into the charity box at the shrine or have to spend it on the truck. There's no end to it."

He finishes his cigarette and gets up.

"Sit still," he says. "I'm going to the quarry."

The boy watches his uncle disappear down the road and wonders why he's going to the quarry.

The boy doesn't know what to do. He climbs up inside the truck and sits behind the wheel, his legs barely reaching the pedals. He turns the steering wheel right and left as far it will go. Then he studies the gauges. He knows them all. The speedometer, the gas gauge, the temperature gauge. He switches the lights on and off. Then he thinks of trying the engine—maybe by some miracle from the Imam-zadeh it will start. But there's only a *tick, tick* from the starter. He sinks back into the old seat stained with grease and smelling of gasoline and thinks he doesn't want to be a truck driver anymore. Feeling tired and exhausted, he falls asleep. When he wakes up, he opens the door and jumps down.

The old shrine sits dust-covered and sad-looking among the boulders, its black banner hanging limp. Beside it, the front end of the brown truck lies low under its burden of stones like a tired camel that has knelt down with its neck stretched out along the ground.

It will be night soon, the boy thinks, and what will he do then? But at the moment he tells himself he will follow the road and head for the horse center at Baaj-ga, in the dying light he sees someone coming up the pass carrying a sack. When the figure gets closer, he puts down the sack and wipes the sweat from his brow. The boy recognizes his uncle and runs toward him, but his uncle waves to him to stop.

"Careful, Tohamtan," he says. "Be careful."

The boy doesn't understand at first and then sees the bold red writing on the side of the sack. "Dangerous," it reads, "Handle with Care."

He watches his uncle, who wipes his brow once more and after staring at the truck and then at the Imam-zadeh, picks up the sack and comes closer.

SHIREEN

Omran, released from his twelve-hour shift at the sugar factory, bicycled home whistling, happy that he finally succeeded in smuggling out a cup of sugar. The narrow dirt road leading to the outskirts of town was damp from an early afternoon shower. Mud glued itself to the tires and rims and accumulated around the brake calipers, making it difficult to pedal. He had to stop repeatedly to scrape off the mud with the stick he kept in a small sack attached to the back rack. He thought it would have been easier to leave the bike at the factory and walk the four miles home—his coworkers who had walked were probably home by now. But he'd decided to take the bike to show Nasreen how he managed to outfox the guards at the gate who searched every conceivable place when the men left the factory at the end of their shifts. Workers lost their jobs for trying to take sugar out, no matter the amount, even if it was the ration they were given to have with their tea.

Omran pictured the surprised look on Nasreen's face when she saw the sugar, but he was nervous as well, thinking someone may have seen him. He tried not to think about it and concentrated on the slippery road, pedaling faster.

He considered himself lucky to have the seasonal job at the sugar factory. It was especially good in the wintertime when there weren't many jobs available. Production began in mid-fall, when sugar beets came to the factory from farms throughout the province, and lasted until early spring. For years he'd tried to get a job at the factory. Then, just after he got married, a neighbor who worked there and knew the ropes gave him a hint. Omran took his advice and during the summer fattened a small lamb that he gave to his neighbor to take to the foreman at the factory. He got the job and, with the money he saved, bought a used Hercules bicycle and some wool Nasreen wove into two small carpets. One went to the foreman, so Omran could be sure of having the job next season. With this year's savings, God willing, he thought, there wouldn't be any extra expenses, and if he didn't spend a coin unnecessarily, he could buy a sewing machine for Nasreen—not a used one, he had promised her, but a shining new Singer she could show off to the neighbor women. Any money left over would go toward the expenses for the baby on the way.

He was halfway home when the sun went behind the distant mountains and the shimmers disappeared from the shallow puddles of rainwater on the road. He felt the chill in his fingers when he stopped to clean the mud off the bicycle. His plan was not to say a word to Nasreen about the sugar until they'd finished dinner. Then he would unscrew the bike seat and ask her to spread a sheet on the floor. He was sure she would be happy and proud of his cleverness watching the sugar pour out of the tube of the bike as he held it upside down.

Nights after dinner, Omran worked on his bike, oiling the chain, checking the brakes, and tightening the loose spokes. Later, he and Nasreen would lie in bed talking. She would tell him about her day, how the baby had behaved inside her, or how his mother or some neighbor woman came to visit and filled up her ears with advice. Then she would ask him about his day at the sugar factory. She was always interested in what went on inside the factory and loved to hear him tell how sugar beets were turned into sugar. He did his best to describe how the truckloads of beets were first dumped into a huge pit and tossed and turned as high-pressure water hoses washed and pushed them through the slicer machine that shredded them into a mass of strings carried by conveyor belt and dumped into the belly of the big rotating drum called a diffuser. After the diffuser cooked them in hot water and steam and extracted their sweetness, the watery juice would be purified, filtrated, and evaporated until at the end the dark-brown molasses was poured into centrifuges and—voilà—turned into white sugar crystals. At this point, Omran would prop himself up on his elbow and look at Nasreen, who seemed as though she could taste the sweetness and would say she bet the fresh sugar would make very tasty shireeni.

That evening, like other evenings, he washed up and they ate dinner, but things didn't turn out the way he imagined. Nasreen was surprised all right to see how cleverly he managed to bring the sugar out, but she was unhappy, and not just unhappy but mad. It wasn't worth it, she told him, and besides it was stealing, and she wasn't going to make any sweets and cakes with stolen sugar—it would affect the baby. She faulted him for being careless and risking the job it had been so hard to get, and just when they were going to have a baby. He argued it wasn't stealing since it was his own ration and he should have the right to do whatever he wanted with it.

They passed the evening without any further words between them until they went to bed and Omran, not wanting to worry her, promised he wouldn't do it again.

But it wasn't easy for Omran to keep his promise. The closer the baby got, the more anxious he became and the more he thought about the traditional sweets made from grain, oil, and sugar that pregnant women should have at the time of the birth. The sweets were vitalizing and nutritious and he would hate for Nasreen to be deprived of them. The first time he'd taken sugar out had gone so well he thought he could do it as many times as he wanted, especially after his hours had rotated to the second shift and the dark of night was to his advantage. During his break, he sneaked out to where the bicycles were parked, unfastened the bike seat with a wrench, poured the sugar inside the tube, and fastened the seat back on. But rather than taking the sugar home, he took it to his mother's, at the other end of the town. His mother wouldn't question him, thinking it was his ration. Omran explained that the sugar was to make the traditional sweet cakes for Nasreen when the delivery got closer.

When the piercing sound of the factory's steam whistle announced the end of the shift, Omran got on his bike and joined his coworkers. They pedaled across the factory yard to the main gate to be checked and let out. He usually tried not to hurry or look suspicious and felt it was safer to stay close to the end of the line, since by the time the guards got to the last few workers they were so anxious to finish they practically pushed everyone out the gate. But today he wanted to get home as quickly as he could. All through his shift he'd been thinking about Nasreen and the baby due to be born any day now. When it was his turn, the guard told him to stand aside. He thought he would be asked a few questions and then sent on his way, since every once in a while the guards liked to pick on someone. After all the other workers were gone, the guard came over with a wrench, grinned at Omran, and banged the wrench against the bike so hard he jumped. The guard took the bike, hit it again at different places and listened. Then he started to unfasten the seat. He spoke as if he weren't addressing Omran, but talking to himself. Strange things happen once in a while, he said. Once in a while someone gets a crazy idea and thinks he's clever, but he forgets that we have our clever ways as well. We have eyes that watch eyes, he said, I'm sure you get my point. When he turned and looked at Omran, the whites of his eyes shone in the glare of the lamp above the gate. You may not believe me, he went on, but nothing goes out of this gate unnoticed or without our getting a taste of it, if you get my meaning.

Omran waited in silence, not really listening but thinking about Nasreen and how worried she'd be if he were late. Finally the seat was off. The guard handed the seat and the wrench to Omran and then threw the beam of his flashlight inside the tube. He bent down, stared inside the small opening, and then, grumbling, turned the bike upside down and shook it. Nothing came out. Well, the guard said, we had a hunch something fishy was going on, but now—he smiled at Omran—everything is clear. Omran nodded, fastened the seat back on the bike, and was about to go through the gate when the guard turned to him. I heard you're going to be a father, he said. Congratulations. That's great, the guard went on. It's a joy being a father. Omran smiled and nodded before hopping on the bike.

He pedaled away at a fast pace, wondering who could have ratted on him. It hit him hard that there were people like that among his coworkers. He had to be watchful and give no excuse to anyone, but at the same time he thought it didn't matter and was relieved he had taken enough sugar.

By the time he got to town, dawn was breaking. A few trucks with loads of sugar beets were heading for the factory. Along the main street, vendors were setting up to offer breakfast. The smell of steaming turnips and freshly baked tea cakes made his mouth water, but he pedaled away. When he reached the alley, he saw a woman come out of his house, head the opposite way up the alley, and disappear from view. He hurried to the gate, pushed it open, and entered the yard. Light was leaking out through the cracks of the door to their room. He propped the bike against the wall and went in. The room was warm and filled with the aroma of cinnamon from the sweet cakes. Nasreen was in bed asleep, her face pale but beautiful. His mother came in from the next room and he noticed she had taken off the mourning clothes she'd worn since the death of his father more than a year ago and was wearing a light-green dress and flowered scarf.

"Oh, my goodness, you're home," she said, kissing him. "Congratulations, my son. Mashallah, you're the father of a healthy little girl and I am a happy grandmother." She stepped into the next room and came back with a small bundle that she put against his chest, a small thing wrapped in a blanket.

Omran stared at the tiny round face, afraid to touch her with his calloused finger. He thought it was a new day for all of them and wondered if he would be able to be a good father and do what was necessary.

"Hi, Shireen, little one," he said to the baby. Then he turned to Nasreen. "Shireen is a nice name, don't you think? Can we call her Shireen?"

"Sure." Nasreen smiled. "I like that."

FAST FRIENDS

Majid and Karim had been good friends since their days in high school and managed to stay friends even though they had quite different personalities. Karim had always been a solitary, middle-of-the road kind of person, while Majid was sociable and a risk-taker. And anytime Karim wouldn't go along with whatever Majid was up to, he would say, "Karim, let's face it, you're just wimpy, and may never change. What else can I say?"

Late one morning after a long night at Majid's house, Karim woke up to the sound of his friend's coughing, but had no energy to get out of bed. It was as if soldiers were marching inside his head. After the nights when Majid showed his hospitality by offering him Afghan opium and homemade vodka, mornings were like this. Karim could tell that Majid was feeling worse than he was from the way he was coughing and arguing with his wife. This kind of activity was routine for Majid, while for Karim it was only a once-in-a-while thing. For one thing, he was always afraid the Morality Squad would rush in and the result would be public lashing and humiliation. The other thing was that he couldn't manage his tiredness afterward and still do his job at the town hall.

Karim suddenly realized he was late for work and got out of bed as quietly as possible so he could sneak away before Majid saw him. He knew his friend would insist on having breakfast and dropping him off at his office on the way to the jewelry shop. If Karim said he was late, Majid would laugh. "Come on, man," he would say, "for God's sake. Do you always have to worry about that job of yours? What's the worst that could happen? That the city sweepers won't go out sweeping?" Karim knew that by the time they finished breakfast, stopped first at the bank and then here and there exchanging pleasantries with friends and acquaintances, it would be almost noon. "Is my watch right?" Majid would say. "How time flies, it's almost lunchtime. Let's go to the shop and order lamb kabab and I promise I'll take you to your office afterward." Often one or two friends would join them.

Over the years, the jewelry store had become a place for people who liked to hang out with Majid—and not many of them were his friends either, the way Karim saw it. Sometimes when Karim got frustrated with the summer heat or the demands of people coming to the Planning Office to request this or that, he would sneak out of work and join them. They would sit enjoying the fruit juice or ice cream that Majid would order from the shop down the street and talk about schemes in the currency market and the price of gold and silver. Always there was news of people leaving the country—many of them after getting into trouble with the law. When they wanted to keep information from Karim, they had a way of talking without giving anything away. Someone's name would come up and Karim would hear one of them say, "Ah, yes, no worries . . . he'll be drinking cold water for a while." That meant the person was in jail. Or, "So-and-so's watching the night stars." That was a sign that the person had made it safely to a foreign land. Karim suspected they were involved in the black market for antiquities robbed from the ancient graves or stolen from archeological sites or even from museums with the help of guards who were paid to look the other way.

Karim had read that artifacts smuggled out of this region close to the Persian Gulf found their way across the water to the United Arab Emirates and from there to Europe or North America. He knew about the extraordinary views of the first prime minster of the Islamic Republic, who had gone on record saying it was better for antiquities to leave the country and be someplace they're valued than to stay here and be melted into rings and necklaces.

FAST FRIENDS

One afternoon, Karim found Majid alone in the shop. As they
talked, he had the feeling Majid was about to tell him something—
maybe something he'd heard or some sort of plan he'd made. Majid
had lowered his voice and was watching the front of the shop when
an older man came in and Majid stopped talking. The man was well
dressed and his white beard was nicely trimmed. He seemed to be a
professional of some sort, and Karim could see he wasn't local. He
looked around at the jewelry and then in the display case without
saying a word, then took off his watch and asked Majid to change
the battery. Majid examined the watch with admiration. "A nice
one," he said. The man nodded and smiled. Majid handed back
the watch and said that he didn't have the right kind of battery, but
would be able to get it in a few days. The man said he'd come back,
thanked Majid, and briefly looked Karim's way before leaving.
Karim was thinking about what had just happened, knowing that
Majid never changed batteries on watches and finding it unusual
that Majid, who always judged a person one way or the other,
didn't say a word after the man had gone. Then a woman walked
in. She was conservative-looking, dressed in a full black chador that
she held so only half her face was visible. Majid went over to show
her some jewelry. Karim thought about the years before the Islamic
Revolution, when Majid first opened his shop and young women
in short sleeves and miniskirts, their black hair loose around their
shoulders, would come in and Majid in his charming way would
interest them in buying something.

Those were the days, thanks to the oil money, when their town
started down the road of modernization and expansion. Majid was
one of the lucky ones who'd been successful in real estate and made a
name for himself. By some miracle, or more likely greed, a parcel of
land, sometimes without even being seen, would change hands a few
times within a short period of time, its price going up and up. Majid
was always ahead of his competition, thanks in part to information
Karim was able to provide him from the town hall—unannounced
information such as what zones were to receive water or electrical or
telephone lines, where and when new streets and roads were going
to be constructed, and so on. A few years later, when the real estate

market was losing air, Majid hinted he was going to take his money out, and Karim agreed. Not long after, protests against the Shah's regime escalated all over the country and angry people burned down cinemas and banks. Karim said the currency would turn to ashes in their hands and it was time to buy gold, which Majid did. Then he went into the jewelry business and opened a shop near the city center with the catchy name of Tela Foroshy Zarnegar—Zarnegar Jewelry. Since "zarnegar" means goldsmith and can also be a surname, people started to call him Mr. Zarnegar.

Karim never asked Majid for anything in return for the favors he did, but always enjoyed Majid's friendship and generosity. Majid's door was always open to him and he often invited Karim to accompany him on his travels to the islands in the Persian Gulf or the Arab countries. Or, before the revolution, to a polo match at the horse center. Majid always encouraged Karim to go into business with him and would pester him about it. "I know you don't care about earthly things," he would say, "things that would keep you from becoming a Sufi or whatever it is you're doing."

He was right about that. For years, Karim had been trying to be on the path of Sufism, reading Rumi, Attar, and other mystic poets and trying to live like a dervish, in a simple righteous way, without attachments. It wasn't easy, but he hadn't totally given up.

"I still can't see it," Majid would tease him. "It's not in you to wear a white robe and cap and wander the desert whirling until you dissolve in time and place. Couldn't you try for a change and join me in the jewelry business? We could open another shop and you would be out of that decaying office of yours. It would be fun and you'd meet different kinds of people." Then he would laugh. "And who do you think is most interested in jewelry? Women, my friend." Karim would shake his head, but Majid would go on ribbing him, saying he would eventually have a stroke working in the basement of the town hall or, worse, would go bald like his boss.

Majid convinced the woman who'd come into his shop to buy an expensive necklace, and a pair of earrings and bracelets to go with it. After she left, he sat down with a big smile to eat his melted ice cream. He said she was the wife of a rich merchant and was shopping for her son's fiancée. Just as he was saying he expected her to come back for more jewelry, a skinny young man in work clothes came in. He approached the desk, pointed to the telephone, and asked if he could make a short phone call. He said he had an air conditioner for Mr. Moradi, who lived in the apartment above the store but hadn't answered the door.

Majid pushed the telephone over to him. "Moradi's traveling," he said. "And who knows when he'll be back."

"He's traveling?" the young man said with a twitch in his brow. "Then why did they send me to install a unit for him?" He dialed a number. "Hello," he said after a second. "Mr. Moradi didn't open his door . . . I'm calling from Mr. Zarnegar's jewelry store. He says that Moradi is traveling. I see . . . Okay, well . . . What should I do then, bring the unit back? . . . Okay, I'll ask . . . Okay, bye."

He put down the receiver. "It looks like the company made a mistake and sent me a day early. My boss is asking, if it isn't any trouble, could we leave the unit here until tomorrow. Mr. Moradi should be back then. I'll be here when you open the shop in the morning."

"The old man is never home," Majid said grumbling. "And whenever there's something for him, it gets left here. I've become a storage room for him, and now this air conditioner—can you believe it?"

"Sorry for troubling you, Mr. Zarnegar," the young man said. "Mr. Moradi has been waiting for this for a long time. I am afraid if I return it, another customer will take it. I'm sure you're aware of the shortage of cooling units and the heatwave we're facing."

Majid laughed softly. "My dear man, where do you think I can keep it? I have customers coming in here."

The man pleaded and Majid agreed and said they should hurry, because he was about to close up for the day and he better come and take it out of there whether Moradi is back or not.

"Thank you, Mr. Zarnegar. Of course. I'll be here before you are," he said and dashed out of the store, unloaded a big crate from the pickup with the help of a coworker, and left it in the corner of the shop.

"This huge unit is for Moradi?" Majid said, looking at the crate. "For that small apartment of his?"

"You know," Karim said, "I could use an air conditioner like this in my house." The words came out of his mouth before he could think.

Majid nodded thoughtfully and said if Karim wanted, they could come later that night and take it to his place. "How can they prove they even brought it here?" he asked.

Karim said he was only joking, that he couldn't do that to old man Moradi. Then he tried to change the subject and said that Majid, with all his cleverness, was mistaken about the jewelry or Persian carpet business because the real money was in cooling units, for two reasons. One was that the government had banned all imports. And second, didn't he realize what a heatwave they'd been having in the last few years in their desert town?

Majid jumped on this. "Yes, you're right. When should we start?"

Karim's answer, as usual, was that he wasn't interested. Then Majid, out of nowhere, said that everything had its time, that he was tired and needed a change, and any day he might say goodbye to it all and get out of this desert town and the hellish heat. Then he was quiet and looked at Karim and then away. Karim could see he was debating whether he should say more.

"I have a chance," Majid said finally, lowering his voice, "to get my hands on something, something that if I succeed in getting it away from a few wolves—well, I could buy this town."

Karim thought perhaps this was what Majid was going to tell him earlier.

Then Majid, as if he'd made a mistake and said too much, burst into laughter. "You believe anything I say, don't you? My friend, you've never had a knack for business. And maybe that's a good thing, since there are all sorts of shrewd people in this town who wouldn't blink at taking the shirt off your back."

That evening over dinner at his house, Majid kept talking about the air conditioner. "Come on, Karim, let's do it. Let's go and take it to your place. You can keep it if you want, otherwise I know someone who would love to have it."

Karim wondered whether Majid was really serious about going and getting this cheap air conditioner. And he listened to him going about how they shouldn't worry about Moradi, that he'd gone north and was enjoying the cool air on the Caspian shore and hadn't lost his mind to come back south to the desert heat. He might even have left the country without letting anyone know. And so much was happening in town, no one would give a damn about an air conditioner. He kept nagging Karim, saying he didn't have any sense of adventure.

"Majid," Karim said, "you're driving me crazy. I don't really want the air conditioner, but if you want to store it at my place and then take it away, let's do it."

"There you go, my friend. I knew you had some guts."

Karim started to gather the vodka bottle and the opium pipe, but was stopped by Majid telling him to leave everything as it was.

"What if the Morality Squad walks in?" Karim said. "With your wife asleep in the other room."

"You really surprise me, Karim. If something like that could get me in trouble, I would have been publicly lashed and thrown in jail long ago. Don't you know I have them in the palm of my hand? I know their history, my friend—who they are and where they come from. Sure I don't trust them. They'll stab you in the back, but not me, for something like this, all you have to know is how to deal with them . . . Don't worry—let's go."

They got to the store, and as Majid was about to open the lock, Karim heard a noise and tapped him on the shoulder. They saw someone approaching along the dark sidewalk. "Well, well," Majid said. "Look who is coming by. Excellent brother Mohsseni."

Panicked, Karim took a step back, afraid that the Komiteh guard would smell alcohol on his breath. Images of lying on a bench in the middle of the square and the cracking of the whip took shape in his head. The guard shifted the rifle on his shoulder. "Salaam, Mr. Zarnegar," he said. "I recognized you from afar. What are you doing here so late at night?"

"We've come to see how reliable you are protecting people's property. Impressive indeed. The thief hasn't climbed up the wall and here is the authority to catch him." Then they burst into laughter.

"Are you alone?" Majid asked. "Where's your partner?"

The guard gestured toward the other side of the street, where a shadow and the glow of a cigarette could be seen. Then he looked at Karim and back at Majid, "Is there a problem, Mr. Zarnegar?"

"Oh, no. Not really. You see, this friend of mine"—he turned to Karim—"he gets kind of confused at times. He left something in the store this afternoon and then in the middle of the night remembered it and couldn't wait until morning. And I'm glad you came by, can you give us a hand?—this thing is kind of big."

Karim felt his knees started to go weak and had to put his hand against the wall. Majid unlocked the store. With the help of the guard and his partner, they got the crate in the trunk of the car and they all got in and drove to Karim's house. All the way there, Majid teased them, telling them he bet he could sneak up on them in the dark and disarm them. The guards humored him, saying they knew he could. At the house, they put the crate in the corner of the yard and Karim threw a blanket over it. On the way back, Majid let the guards off at the main street and asked them to come by his shop any time. He would order lemonade and ice cream.

The next morning, when Majid was going to drop Karim off at the town hall, they saw a group of people gathered in front of the jewelry store. A tall man with an athletic figure was cursing the young man who'd left the air conditioner in the shop, yelling at him for bringing the wrong unit, a unit too large for a small apartment. Then, as if getting angrier at seeing Majid, he punched the young man in the mouth, telling him that this was his last job and he was fired.

The young man, blood running down his face, turned to Majid. "Mr. Zarnegar," he said, "please open your shop so that this stupid man takes his air conditioner wherever the hell he wishes."

In the noise and confusion, Karim felt he was hearing Majid's voice from afar. "What are you talking about, dear man," he was saying. "What air conditioner?"

"The one that I left at your store," he pleaded. "That man"—he pointed at Karim—"he was there too."

"Okay, then," Majid said. "Let's take a look and see about this air conditioner of yours." He was about to unlock the store when

Karim burst out. "Yes, that's right," he said to the man, "you did, but we had to take it to my place."

Majid stopped and stared at Karim. "That's right," he turned to the man and spoke in a cool tone. "I told you yesterday that there wasn't enough room in the store. Not knowing if Moradi would show up any time soon, we thought it better to store it at my friend's place. There's no need for fighting and bloodshed. Let's go and you can take it wherever you fancy."

The young man and his boss looked at each other and then at the people who had gathered around. They went over to their pickup, eyeing Majid and Karim and talking in low voices. Karim wondered what was going to happen. After a minute, they indicated they were ready. Majid checked the lock and they left for Karim's house, with the pickup following.

Majid was quiet for a block or two and then pounded the steering wheel with his fist. "What was that you did, man? One drop of blood and you panicked." Karim had never seen him so mad. In fact, he'd never been mad at him. "You should have evaluated the situation first and waited to see what your buddy said or did."

Karim wanted to say he didn't give a damn and why had they done it in the first place anyway? But he knew it wasn't the time. He didn't really care at that point, and just didn't want more trouble. So he kept quiet, hoping they would take the air conditioner and the whole problem would go away.

When they got to the house, the men stayed away, as if anticipating something. Karim opened the gate and stepped into the yard. The first thing he saw was the blanket on the ground, the cardboard box torn and the metal sides of the air conditioner tossed to one side. When he got closer, he could see that metal box was empty. He turned and looked at Majid, who was a few steps behind him. The two men standing at gate turned and ran. It took a minute before Majid yelled out, "My shop, my shop!" The two men were already in their pickup and rushing away.

On the way back to the store, Majid drove fast and kept cursing. "Dammit, you see what happened. I'm doomed—so stupid of me. I failed to see it."

When they got to the shop, Majid jumped out, opened the door, and ran to the store's back room, without a minute's delay. Then he rushed back out. "I'm doomed!" he shouted. "The sons of bitches have taken everything. Everything's gone."

He was yelling and cursing and other shopkeepers and bystanders, hearing the commotion, circled around and tried to calm him down. Karim stood apart, the sun beating on his head and sweat running down his face.

The next day, Majid went to the hospital with chills and a fever. "I'm doomed," he kept saying when Karim and other friends visited him. "My gold, my jewelry—all gone, my future gone." His wife stayed beside his bed, wiping his brow. "My dear Niloofar," he said to her. "I disappointed you. I planned to send you to school after we got married, and help you with your dreams. I failed to do it, and now I've managed to ruin our future as well." She didn't say much and tried to comfort him, telling him not to worry, that it wasn't the time to be upset. She'd always been a quiet woman, a typical wife, Karim often thought, and he knew she'd wanted to go to college, but her religious parents wouldn't let her and married her to Majid. It seemed to Karim that they were happy together, and he wondered if the unfortunate situation would change things for them.

During the week or so that Majid was in the hospital, Karim wondered if his friend would ever again be the cheerful and carefree person he'd always known. But then there were times that nothing was wrong with him—that he wasn't really ill, like it was all a pretense, especially when he would fix his eyes on one spot and murmur, "Everything is gone. I'm doomed." At times like that, Karim almost thought he could discern some sense of satisfaction.

Majid and his wife disappeared the day he was released from the hospital.

That same afternoon, Karim was picked up by the authorities. He was under interrogation for a week, with threats that they'd send him to the center of the province, where they knew how to make people talk. But he repeated the same thing he'd told the police the day they questioned him and Majid. The more he repeated the story of the air conditioner, the more confused he got and the more the truth seemed to get lost—it was the death of the truth, he thought, and falsehoods were taking the shape of truth. He told them he didn't know anything and had no idea what Majid or others were involved in or where Majid had disappeared to. Of course they didn't believe him.

As the days went by, the words of the poet Sa'adi kept coming to him. "One who sits with the crooked people, if he doesn't learn their nature, will be accused of following their ways." He'd been friends with Majid and now he was accused of helping him and Moradi smuggle antiquities out of the country in a scheme masterminded by Majid. He was accused of knowing people like the Shahpourian brothers and others who fled the country, but who didn't know someone out of the country? They thought he had information and demanded details and names. They wanted to know what was inside the fake air conditioner and who the delivery men were and where they'd gone. They accused him of being anti-revolutionary and anti-Islam, of drinking alcohol and trafficking opium.

Karim knew that these sorts of crimes were punishable by public hanging—and knew they'd do it. It had happened to hundreds of people more important than he. He was sure, not because of what they accused him of, but because he knew they were outraged that Majid had outsmarted them by setting up a fake robbery within a fake robbery—something that Karim himself didn't see at first—a scam to take artifacts out of the country and not pay off the authorities who were part of the network helping him. So there he was in jail, trying to understand what had happened, while Majid and his collaborators were somewhere far away "watching the night stars," as Karim had often heard them say.

IN THOSE DAYS

Daavar didn't know what year it was. It didn't matter now, he thought, close to a half century must have passed since that day. He was young then and had just received his teaching certificate and come to teach at the primary school in the small southern town. In those days, the town was a faraway place and hadn't grown to be a big city with paved streets and high-rises. It was a sleepy town, with only one primary school and a factory that made refrigerators and electric fans.

It was almost two years after he started his teaching job that he had a bad automobile accident. The injury to his right leg was a gift from that accident and left him lame. His old automobile was badly damaged. In those days cars ran on gasoline, unlike today. After he was released from the hospital, he had the car towed to a garage on the outskirts of the town to be fixed.

One winter day two or three weeks later, he went to get his car back. The sky looked mercurous and there wasn't much warmth in the afternoon sun. The mechanic asked him to wait since the car wasn't ready. The waiting room was small and closed in, with grease-stained chairs, and smelled of motor oil, cigarettes, and years of neglect. Before his throat could tighten up, he limped to the area behind the garage to get some fresh air. What a prospect. Everywhere there were piles of useless metals, pipes, empty barrels of oil, and worn-out tires of all sizes. All sorts of decaying cars and trucks smashed beyond repair were pushed against one another. A cold wind yowled like the cries of the injured who'd been trapped inside and reminded him of how lucky he'd been to survive his accident. As he walked on, he found himself faced with the decaying skeleton of a huge Caterpillar loader. It stood in his way like a prehistoric being, its broken lights two blind eyes and its loading bucket a big toothless mouth gaping open and ready to grab him.

He was studying this beast when the smell of something burning assaulted his nose and he saw coils of smoke folding up into the air. He went toward the place where the smoke was rising. A small fire was burning in front of an old shack made of aluminum sheets and plywood. There was a tree, the only tree he saw there, a mulberry he thought, with a big trunk and branches extending over the shack. And a small vegetable garden, not more than two meters by two, with most of the plants wilted or dead. Then he saw someone sitting beside the fire. It was a man so small and old that Daavar wondered for a moment whether he was alive. But then he coughed and spoke in a tired voice, as if he hadn't spoken for years.

"Come and sit down, my son," he said, pointing a bony finger toward a piece of cardboard on the ground beside the fire. "Come and warm yourself."

Daavar stepped forward involuntarily. The expression on the old man's face was calm and filled with the need of a companion. He breathed heavily, just the way Daavar did now, struggling to take air into his lungs. Daavar sat down and watched the old man warming up his opium pipe beside the fire. The old man picked up a burning ember with a pair of tongs and blew on it. "I saw you a couple of weeks ago," he said. "When you brought your automobile in for repair. You were in that car and survived?"

Daavar nodded.

"Remarkable. You were lucky." He blew on the ember until the ashes flew away. Then he held it on the pipe's china bulb right above the piece of opium. As he drew on the pipe, bringing the ember close to the opium without touching it, his toothless cheeks caved in and the opium started to vaporize with a slow *jeer-jeer* sound and a soft but bitter smell. He released his breath and some of the smoke fountained out of his nostrils and mouth, making a disintegrating fog in front of his face. He kept smoking until the opium was gone. Then he put the ember down, grabbed the small needle dangling at the end of an elegant chain, and pushed the needle into the tiny hole on the top of the bulb to clean and reopen it. He put another piece of opium on the bulb, picked up another piece of ember, and drew on the pipe, repeating the same performance.

Daavar watched with interest. The old man was like an artist totally cut off from everything and immersed in his own actions. Once in a while he would stop smoking and say a few words. The more Daavar took in the fleeting smoke that came his way, the more lethargic he felt.

"I may be alive for only a few more months or maybe just a few more days," the old man said. "I've lived a long life. It's seemed an eternity. A life that has crawled on. What days, what years, and what didn't I see from people? What didn't I see with these eyes that have hardly any light in them now? Since you've come here, I need to tell you. Maybe a hidden hand has brought you to me so I could tell you what I've kept inside for so long." He stopped talking and raised his head, the fire sparking in his eyes. "Things that have burdened me all my life and that I don't wish to take to the other world with me. I want to tell you because you're a teacher."

Daavar wondered how the old man knew he was a teacher. All at once, the old man sprang up, so agile and energetic it surprised him. He grabbed a pick and shovel that were leaning against the shack and gestured for Daavar to follow him. They walked over to the loader and the old man started to dig out the earth that had accumulated in the corner of the bucket. Then he squatted and worked with his hands until an oxidized hook became visible.

"Take a good look at this," he said. Then he moved to the other end of the bucket, again digging and removing the earth until another hook appeared. "You see these?"

Daavar nodded.

"This equipment is used in construction," he went on. "For digging and removing earth and must be used just for that propose.

The hooks are extra, they were welded to the bucket for a different purpose altogether. You've seen it, now come. Let's go back."

They sat by the fire and the old man warmed up his pipe again. That late afternoon, sitting beside him by the fire, Daavar had the feeling that he wasn't from our human race but was a being from an unknown world that had taken human shape. Every so often, the old man poked the fire with a pair of tongs and then grabbed a new ember, blew on it, and went on smoking his pipe.

"I've put so much behind me," the old man said. "When I was a young lad, there was a horse center down in the valley with beautiful horses. A good family ran the place. I worked there, taking care of the horses. Then I learned to work with a loader and carried hay and oats and barrels of molasses to the stables, things like that, an easy job. A few years later I partnered with a man I worked with and bought this equipment." He pointed to the loader. "I contracted to work at the factory where they made refrigerators, fans, and other household things. The loader was our livelihood and we struggled for years until we paid off the money we'd borrowed. We were just about to have an easier time—'to drink a glass of water in peace' as they say—but no, another disaster had to happen and change everything."

The old man went on smoking and talking and some of the smoke crept toward Daavar, who inhaled involuntarily, trying to prepare himself for whatever the old man was driving at.

"Anyway, maybe my partner was innocent in this, I don't know. He wasn't a stupid or hateful person. I guess they made him do it. In those days, if an order came from some government authority, you had to obey it, you had no other choice. You should know that in those days, ghanoon va mas-oliat sefr—regulations and accountability were zero. It was a strange time. After so many years of problems, all because of the incompetent people in charge, the infected wound had opened and irrationality and cruelty were the first outcome. Ruthlessness became the norm. I don't think there's anyone my age to remember what we went through. Well, let that be. I was going to tell you about the incident in the center of town—an awful thing my partner was involved in. I was so angry I wished his death. I'm

78

sorry to say that, but he participated in something vah-shat-naak—
something atrocious. In those days that kind of cruelty was seen
all over the country. There were new laws and inhumane ways of
punishing people, but this was the first time in our town and I was
indirectly involved, and I would say a victim as well. It wasn't some
small forgettable thing, you see, and it changed all our lives."

He poked the fire and grabbed another ember. "What a day it
was for us. The beginning of our downfall. It was high noon and
the heat seemed to have no end to it. I'd gone to the bazaar for
something and saw the rush of people young and old hurrying to
the town square. Now it's surrounded by high-rises, but the tall-
est structure in those days was a three-story building. I followed
them to see what was going on. In those days, there was something
happening almost every day in some corner of town and people
like a herd would go and watch. One day they would be lashing
someone for drinking alcohol, another day punishing someone for
having a party and playing music, or humiliating people in some
way for some petty crime. All punishments were public, suppos-
edly to teach people a lesson. I'll tell you it never worked—look
around, have crime and corruption stopped? Anyway, as I made my
way through the crowd, I saw two men with black hoods over their
heads standing in front of a loader. Their hands were tied behind
their backs and there were towing cables around their necks. The
ends of the cables were attached to the hooks of a loader's bucket.
In that crowd, with all the commotion and the Morality Squad
in charge, I felt deaf and dumb. My eyes were on the two men
who would be dead at any minute and I didn't realize that it was
my loader—you see, it didn't used to have those hooks—until the
engine roared and I saw my partner behind the wheel. It was too
late to do anything, even if I could have. They'd welded the hooks
to the bucket at the factory, and my partner had driven it to the
center of the town. I saw the bucket rising higher and the cables
tightening. I dashed out of there . . . before . . ."

He was quiet and Daavar was shaking inside. He turned his eyes
from the old man, even though he wasn't seeing him clearly and
it was as if he had melted into the darkness. "You won't believe it,

but it was that way in those days, using cranes and loaders to hang people for their crimes. It was happening all over the country. Well, let it be . . ."

Daavar shifted in place and was about to get up and go, but the old man's burning eyes took his courage from him.

"Where are you going? Come on, sit," the old man commanded. "I know I've disturbed you, my son, but sit and be patient. Come, have a smoke to calm you down."

Daavar shook his head.

"Well, I understand that a young man like you and a teacher shouldn't smoke. I do it to keep myself calm. Many people in those days were addicted and are now, I imagine . . . Anyway, after that rooz vahshi—that wild day—I didn't want my equipment to be in town anymore and was terrified it would be used in the same way again, or for some other horrible thing. You see, a year before that incident, a religious leader famous for his outrageous ways assembled a few bulldozers. First they burned the beautiful horse stables down in the valley and then headed for one of our ancient sites, the ruins of Takht-e Jamshid—the Palace of Persepolis—with the aim of bulldozing it. Fortunately, some local people—you know. no matter what, there are always some righteous people around— they stood in his path and stopped him. I heard about it in time and hurried to where my loader was working, terrified that it was being used for this purpose. Not wanting any other crazy thing to happen, I contracted with a company building a highway in the middle of the country, in some faraway desert, and sent the loader and my partner there."

The old man's manner of talking, his silence and the look in his eyes, kept Daavar from diverting his attention, let alone getting up to leave. Slowly they drowned in the evening's darkness until the objects around them lost their familiar shape and look.

"It wasn't more than a week later," the old man went on, "that my partner called, urgently wanting me to go where he was. He said that the loader had gone crazy. I thought that he's the one who had gone crazy—who ever heard of a machine going crazy? A machine isn't human to go crazy. Anyway, he said if I didn't go, he would go away and let everything be buried in the sand of the desert. So, I got a bus ticket and went. He swore that the loader in the middle of the night had turned itself on and driven around in a circle with its lights flashing and its bucket going up and down. I didn't believe him. But I should have. I said, man, maybe someone is trying to scare you so we'll leave this job. He didn't believe that. So I had no choice except to stay and see what was going on. Well, nothing happened the first night. Or the second night. It was the same the third night, and then a week passed with no sign of craziness on the part of the loader or my partner. But I myself was on the verge of going crazy in that bare land all alone and with nothing around. One day I went to the nearby village to buy tea, sugar, and cigarettes and some things for my partner and was planning to go back home after a few days. I don't really know why, except that I was tired, but I decided to stay in the village overnight. The next day when I went to the construction site, I saw a group of workers gathered around the loader. Then I saw an awful sight. The bucket of the loader was high in the air and . . ." The old man paused. ". . . And the body of my partner was hanging from it. The teeth of the bucket were pushed into his ribs."

A chill ran through Daavar as he turned and looked at the loader, which by now was only a shadow in the dark of evening.

"My thinking was that someone, some jealous person, didn't want us to work there," the old man went on. "It even occurred to me that someone from our town, someone related to that horrible incident, had something to do with it . . . But I didn't leave. I stayed—youth can make one do senseless things, you know. I stayed and kept working for a month or so, until another hellish night came my way."

He stopped talking and stared into the darkness and then refreshed his pipe. "I woke up with the roar of the loader. The beam of its headlights flashed into the tent, and I'd barely managed to jump out when its half-raised bucket tore through the tent and took it high up in the air, before dumping it on the ground and running over it. I dashed out of its way, but it started to come after me, its lights going on and off and its bucket rising and falling.

81

These machines can't go very fast, they only have strength and power to tear the earth. But that night it was like it had grown wings. It roared after me. And no matter how fast I ran across the desert, it kept after me. Suddenly it came to me to run in a circle. How many times I circled around, with the damn evil after me, God only knows. Then I made my move. I grabbed the step bar and pulled myself up."

He poked at the fire impatiently.

"Up to that point," he went on, "I was thinking someone was operating the damn thing and trying to do the same thing he'd done to my partner. My aim was to grab whomever it was and throw him in front of the loader, but when I reached across the seat, it was empty. There was no one behind the wheel."

Daavar heard the *jeer-jeer* sound of opium burning as the old man drew forcefully on the pipe. Then he put down the pipe and the tongs.

"Can you believe it?" he said. "The seat empty and the loader running mad like that? But it wasn't the time to be scared and lose myself, you see. I got behind the wheel, but I couldn't control it. It was like some invisible hand had the controls. How long I tried, I can't remember. Then I became aware the loader was standing still and there was no movement and no sound except the hissing sound of the desert. The stars were piercing down from the darkness. My hands were frozen to the wheel and the loader was as quiet as if it had never been turned on. I didn't dare move. I sat there, drenched in sweat, until the sun came up and slowly the compound came alive with workers and the sound of equipment starting."

Daavar was about to say maybe something mechanical or electrical was wrong, but didn't get the chance.

"Afterward," the old man went on, "I was sick with fever and chills for a week in the hottest place on earth. I had no choice but to sweat it out in a tent with no doctor or clinic for hundreds of kilometers. A gypsy man who would come around to sharpen tools gave me some herbal medicine and I think it helped me calm down. After I recovered, I wanted to sell the loader, but no one was interested. Rumor was that it was controlled by the jinns."

The way he turned his head, his face half lit by the fire and his eyes glowing, Daavar thought that if jinns existed, surely this man could be one. Drops of sweat crawled down Daavar's neck and back. He wanted to get out of there, but was afraid that if he made a move, at a sign from the old man, the loader would jump out of the dark and put its teeth into him.

"I poured two handfuls of desert sand into the engine." The old man's dry voice brought Daavar back. "And I said, 'Damn you, it's either you or me.' Then I switched the motor on. It click-clacked and then started to bang until steam rushed out, then it banged one more time and was dead silent. I decided to bring it here. The owner of this land, a kind man, let me build a shack by this tree. The orchard had died because of the years of drought, and only this mulberry tree is left. It was young then, but I've watered it and it's survived and now, as you can see, is old. And who knows, it may keep on living for a long time to come. I can't remember how many years ago it was. After losing everything and not wanting to have anything to do with anybody, I had no place else to go."

Daavar shifted in place, getting ready to leave, realizing he'd forgotten all about his car.

"Where are you going in such a hurry?" the old man said. "Please sit—come, I know I've disturbed you. I'm sorry, but I had to tell you. Because you're a teacher. Come closer, have a smoke before you go so you can relax. I see you're upset. Come."

He held out the pipe toward Daavar. Daavar moved closer and, taking the pipe, followed his guidance.

"Take in the smoke slowly." The old man brought the red ember to the tiny piece of opium sitting on the bulb of the pipe.

The smoke, warm and harsh, passed Daavar's throat and rushed into his lungs.

"That's enough. Now hold your breath—don't waste it."

Daavar kept his mouth shut and tried hard not to cough.

"Good. You did well, like an expert. You'll relax now. Do you know why I put this poison into my blood? It's so I can deal with all the things I've seen in my life. Who says machines don't have souls? I can swear that this loader of mine had one."

He stared into the surrounding darkness as if seeing things Daavar's eyes couldn't discern. Daavar couldn't say how, but somehow before the old man could say something, he was on his feet and limping among the damaged cars, trying to find his way back. After that night he avoided going close to that part of town. He had to avoid the town square as well, since in the confusion of cars, trucks, and people, he would think of the old man and have no choice but to get out of there as fast as he could.

Many years after that night, when Daavar was an old man himself, he decided to take his twelfth-grade students—they had a high school by then—to that part of town. He was sure the old man was long gone, but he thought he might find the junkyard and the loader. They traveled across the city, through crowded streets filled with traffic, the bus starting and stopping endless times—the town had grown tenfold since the night Daavar saw the old man. He had tried to prepare his students for what they might see, but wondered how he could tell them the whole story of that day. It seemed to take a long time to get there and he realized that the city had expanded over the barren area and far beyond. They got off the bus where he thought the junkyard used to be—near the water tower that was still there—but the area was now a green park with trees, flowers, and water fountains.

Limping, he hurried the students up and down the park, passing the strolling young lovers and the old men sitting on benches turning their praying beads and talking and playing backgammon. When they got to the far end of the park, Daavar stood tired and confused, his students looking at him with questioning eyes. He sat on a bench to rest and after a while realized his students had scattered through the park and a few of them were playing soccer with a small plastic ball someone had come up with. He got up and walked among the tall rows of cypresses and past them, entering an area with poplars and weeping willows and pomegranate trees. Then he saw the tree, with its wide trunk and branches reaching in all directions. Was that the old mulberry tree? he wondered. And that figure, that gaunt old figure who came and sat leaning against the tree, was that the old man? He walked toward the tree and wanted to call out to the old man, but no matter how he tried, he couldn't remember his name.

THIS LAME AND STUBBORN MULE

The radio was pounding out patriotic marching music—trumpets, cymbals, and drums accompanying a chorus of Persian and Arabic revolutionary verses. It had become routine, starting at seven o'clock every morning. He turned the radio off and heard a vague muffled sound that he couldn't place but thought must be heavy trucks slowly moving through the city. He finished his breakfast and was about to clear the table when a sudden gust of wind twisted the young tree in the yard and thunder rattled the window. Soon the rain started to fall.

A spring shower, he thought, what a nice surprise. He glanced at the wall clock and decided to hurry so he could get some fresh air on the way to school. He took the dishes to the sink and set them on top of the ones from last night's dinner, then wiped off the table and looked around. The stove was off and the lights were out. He put on his raincoat and picked up his umbrella and his briefcase with the exam papers he had graded the night before.

He reached for the doorknob, but it wouldn't turn. He tried again. It wouldn't move. He gave it more force, twisting and pulling, but couldn't get the door to open. He was sure the knob opened clockwise but tried the opposite way, just in case, turning harder. It was no use. He stepped back and stared at the door. Then he put down his briefcase and, with the umbrella still under his arm, grabbed the doorknob with both hands, turning, tugging, and pulling. The door shook violently in its frame but didn't open. It was as if the knob hadn't turned for years.

He put the umbrella on top of his briefcase and went to the window. Rain was drumming on the glass. He grabbed the latch and tried to open the window. It wouldn't budge. He pushed as hard as he could. His fingers turned white with pain, but the latch didn't show the slightest sign of moving.

Now he was worried. It seemed impossible to understand what was happening. Yesterday afternoon when he came home, he had unlocked the door with no problem and left the window open to air out the room.

He looked into the yard. The wind and rain had picked up and the young tree was twitching so vigorously that he thought it would snap. The same vague muffled sounds rumbled in the distance. The ticking of the clock reminded him that it was getting late. Soon the school bell would call the students to their classrooms and his class would be there awaiting him.

He turned from the window and went back to the door, determined to open it. He gripped the knob with both hands and tried to turn it so vigorously that a sharp pain ran through his wrist. Agitated, he rubbed his wrist and went to the window. He hit the latch with his fist a few times without paying attention to the increasing pain in his hand. The latch held fast.

He dashed into the kitchen and returned with a hammer. He hit the doorknob. It wouldn't move. He hammered harder. The knob bent without turning. At the window, he hit the latch. Easy at first and then harder, but it didn't move. Then he aimed at the glass, hitting as hard as he could. The hammer bounced back and raindrops on the opposite side of the glass flew away. Baffled, he stared at the glass. The web of water flowing down the windowpane took shape again. It can't be, he thought, moving his hand over the cold glass showing not the slightest crack.

Then, looking around the room and not knowing what to do, he noticed the telephone on his desk and rushed for it. When he picked up the receiver, there was no dial tone. The line was dead. His hand shook as he put the receiver down. He backed away from the desk until he was up against the wall and stood there, his arms limp at his sides.

Am I asleep? Am I dreaming? he wondered. He could hear the ticking of the clock. He looked from the door to the window to the desk. This is my apartment, he told himself, there's my desk and the bookshelf with my mother's picture on top. My briefcase and umbrella are by the door where I left them. It's like any morning when I get ready to go to school and meet my students. They're waiting for me. He looked at the clock. I should have been there a half hour ago.

He walked across the room and tripped over the hammer lying on the floor. Who could he tell about what was happening? Who would believe him? He could see the principal narrowing his eyes and flashing his devilish smile. "Give us a break, my dear Mr. Ghaedi," he would say. "What do you take us for?" The old math teacher might be more sympathetic. He usually had something thoughtful to say. "I've seen plenty in this land of ours," he would say in his dry voice. "Anything is possible. Anything." Then, in a whisper, he would add his advice. "My dear lad, one must be crafty to a mathematical precision nowadays. Trust no one, and always beware of your landlord. Landlords are always on the watch. Never advance a controversial point of view about them, especially to your young students."

The ticking of the clock was deafening. It was too late, he thought. The school bell would have rung by now and his students would be sitting on the old wooden benches waiting. He rushed to the door and grappled with the handle, then flew to the window and struggled with the latch. It was no use. He walked around the room and without thinking turned the radio on. The same music—military or patriotic, he couldn't tell—was playing. He turned it off.

He sat at the desk and wiped the sweat from his forehead. His temples were throbbing. He thought he heard a door open and close and jumped up and rushed toward the window. "Help . . .

Help!" he cried out as loudly as he could. "Is anyone there?" He brought one ear close to the window and listened. There was only the dripping rain and the ticking of the clock. Outside, the sky was getting darker and he could still hear the humming of heavy trucks. He told himself to be patient and remain calm. He had read somewhere that the most frightening thing can be the fear in your mind. He should control himself and give his heart and mind a rest. Why not lie down for a while?

He walked to the bedroom, stretched out on the bed with his raincoat on, and stared at the ceiling. Maybe someone was playing a joke on him, but who? He didn't socialize much and his neighbors in this old part of town seemed to be compliant citizens who would try not to do anything out of the ordinary, certainly not the old widower next door who was sick and showed signs of increasing weariness. He wondered if the old man's son, who had managed to leave the country not long ago, was okay wherever he'd gone. When was it that the old man, seeing him in the alley, had opened up to him? Their conversation had never gone beyond the usual greetings, but one day out of the blue he spoke to him. "Mr. Ghaedi," he said. "My son is gone. He was able to find a way to leave. You, young man, should try to leave as well. You never know what's in the air around here. Find a way and go while you're in the spring of your life. Anyone with any sense left long ago."

Then there was the bank clerk and his wife who lived on the other side. Did they have anything to do with this situation? He hadn't seen the wife recently. Nice lady—thoughtful. She brought him turnip soup last winter when he had that bad cold. She'd browsed the titles on his bookshelf and said she and her husband had worked for a local newspaper before it was closed down by the Department of Guidance. She gave him a look that made clear her feelings about the things that were happening in their city.

He rose and sat on the edge of the bed, wondering who would be able to help him.

"The garbageman," he said out loud. "Of course, the garbageman."

His voice sounded odd, as if it were only an echo. The garbageman would come like any other day and, when there was no trash can outside the gate, would ring the bell. That had happened before, why not today? Then he'd go to the window and call out as loudly as he could to get his attention. The garbageman would climb the wall and jump down into the yard. He reflected for a moment. No, the garbageman was too fat to climb the wall. He couldn't even jump over a trash can if it happened to roll across his path.

Who else could help? he again asked himself.

The school janitor—yes, the school janitor. He was tall and skinny and could certainly climb the wall. He was sure the class monitor would go to the principal and say he hadn't shown up. And then the principal would call him. He looked at the phone beside the bed and picked up the receiver. It was still dead. He assured himself that the principal would find out that the phone wasn't working and would send the school janitor after him. He'd done it before, like the morning not long ago when he had been glued to the TV and had forgotten all about school, watching the river of young men and women flooding the streets of the capital carrying banners, waving flags, and chanting, "Where's my vote?" That many young people together and so suddenly. All united in their demands. How did it happen? He never thought he'd see it in his lifetime. Was the silence finally broken? But then things went quiet as fast as they started.

The outside cold was slowly finding its way in, but he paid no attention. He got up and walked to the living room and turned on the TV. To his surprise, it only hissed and flickering white sparks floated on the screen. He decided to occupy himself with something else and pulled out a book from the shelf. It was the odes of Hafez, and he let it fall open.

> *Again the Zephyr spreads musk with its breeze*
> *The old world rejuvenated, if you please*

The familiar lines puzzled him. He loved Hafez and the way his poetry triggered perplexity in the mind. Ha, he thought, the clever poet did it again, sending me the Zephyr to awaken my thoughts. He pushed the book back in its place and sat down at his desk. He took out a sheet of paper. "This morning," he wrote vigorously, "like other mornings, I was getting ready to go to school, when . . . when this phenomenon . . . this . . ." He hesitated, distracted by the images of his students in his mind. Then he pushed the paper and everything else off the table and dumped out the exam papers from his briefcase on top of the desk. Last night when he was correcting them, one after another they had brought a smile to his lips and made him feel proud. One particular answer to the question "Explain the situation of living in a landlocked country" had made him laugh out loud. "Living in a landlocked country," the pupil had written, "is like taking a shower in a bathroom that has no windows. The steam will rise and rise and you won't be able to see anything and it will get hotter and hotter." He remembered the student, a tall, skinny kid who was well liked by his classmates and enjoyed entertaining the class and making everyone laugh.

It was the best class he'd had in some years. They were smart and asked clever questions. The exams showed the result of their efforts, and now at this moment they were waiting to get them back.

He picked up an exam and glanced at it, then turned it over and looked at the other side. Paper in hand, he stared into space and imagined the schoolboys at their desks. He was calling them one by one and handing them their papers. Then he addressed the class and talked about history, since many of the exam questions were about history. "We, at this time and this moment in history, are making history," he said. "History is not about this war and that, who lost and who won. Or about this king and that prince. History is nothing except our activities. Our forebears made history by living and doing what needed to be done and we are continuing. It's an onward process. Like a vehicle that carries us forward. In some countries, this vehicle travels as fast and smooth as a plane. In others, it's strong and rough like a locomotive. And in this ancient land of ours, history moves with the slowness of a lame and stubborn mule." The schoolboys laughed. "Yes, we in this corner of the world are riding our lame, tired mule, sometimes dozing off and many times, rather than facing ahead, turning back and amusing ourselves with our ponderous past that keeps following us—a past filled with the ruins of castles, forts, and shrines that cover our ancient land like decayed teeth." The boys looked at him, their black eyes open wide. "And this stubborn mule not only keeps throwing us on the ground, but kicks us right in the chest and so hard"—the class laughed more loudly—"that we twist and turn in pain. But we, more stubborn than this lame mule, rise up each time, covered in blood, dust, and dirt, and mount the mule again. Holding tightly to the old saddle and whipping and shouting, we urge the animal on . . . Attar, the Sufi mystic, wandered with his donkey across the seven cities of love, but we haven't guided ours through the gate of the first town." The students' laughter rose up beyond the walls of the classroom.

Another thunderbolt rattled the window and pellets of rain bounced hard against the glass. His own voice and the laughter of the boys dissipated into space. He got up and faced the door, then grabbed the knob and pulled vigorously a few times. At the window he struggled with the latch. "Is anyone there?" he cried out. "Help . . . Help . . . Where is everyone?"

He put his forehead against the glass and looked out. The yard and the garden were overflowing with rainwater.

He was sitting in the corner of the room, shrouded in dust and hugging his knees. The walls around him were pockmarked with holes and places where chunks of plaster had been hacked off. It looked like someone with a machine gun had taken aim at the walls. The exam papers were scattered all around. The bookshelf lay on its side with all the books thrown out. An upended chair was in the middle of the room. Everything was covered with a dusting of plaster. He didn't know how long he had pounded on the walls. None of his neighbors had responded. Had they gone deaf, moved away, or died?

He stood up and walked around the room, avoiding the chair and the piles of books. The exam papers rustled under his feet. He stopped to look at the picture of his students on his desk. He didn't know when it was taken, but it was one of his earlier classes. They were in front of the anthropology museum on a sunny day and he was standing in the midst of his students. At the museum, they had walked up the spiral stairway depicting the progress of humans from the early days when people gathered in caves to modern times when they lived in skyscrapers.

The more he looked at the picture, the more he thought about two students in particular. One was an introverted boy who kept to himself. His family had moved out of the city and he never saw him again, but years later he learned that he had gone to a university in Tehran to study pre-med and had ended up in America, at a university in California. He was pleased he remembered the student's name was Parviz and also remembered the bewildered look in his eyes, a look that made him wonder how this shy and sensitive student would be able to handle the harshness of life that might come his way. The other student, whose name was Behnam, loved to read and would seek his advice on books and borrowed fiction by contemporary writers. Behnam studied with determination and ended up going to America as well, to study engineering. He looked carefully, and he thought he recognized them among all the students. He walked around the room and then stopped to look at the picture again, noticing that the happy smiling faces of the students had taken on a ghostly appearance.

He started to circle the room again, the ticking of the clock pounding in his head. He held his hand to his ears for a moment before throwing the hammer across the room toward the clock. Shattering glass flew out over the papers and books scattered on the floor. The ticking ceased, and the hands of the clock hung loose, pointing to the center of the earth.

He didn't know how long he'd kept his eyes on the broken clock when he heard a thunk. And then another. It was coming from behind the wall of his neighbor's apartment. He searched wildly for the hammer, then rushed to the wall and banged on it, holding his breath. A moment later there was a louder thunk. He immediately responded, pounding harder. The answer came in a series of heavier thumps. Then he heard another loud blow coming from the direction of his other neighbor. Frantic, he threw himself to the opposite side of the room and brought the hammer down.

A loud blow echoed in response. He pounded again, harder this time, then rushed to the other wall, hitting it madly and stopping only to listen for a response. It seemed the sounds were coming from all directions, all across the neighborhood, from the air and from the streets. Was the whole city crashing down? After a while, exhausted and out of breath, he sat down in the midst of the wreckage, listening and watching the dust settle, encouraged that some communication had started at last.

PART TWO

TRAFFIC LIGHTS

He stared for several minutes before switching off the maquette. The circles of light faded away, but their colors—red, yellow, and green—still penetrated his consciousness.

For more than a month the trouble with the lights had disturbed his work and life. He stepped away from the maquette of the traffic system assembled on the large table in the middle of the lab and looked at the flowchart on the computer monitor. Damn it, he thought, what the hell could be wrong? There's no problem during testing, but then they malfunction at the intersections.

He and his team had reviewed the programs line by line, followed the flowchart step by step, and tested the system over and over. But when the programs were installed, after a couple of hours they would stop functioning and throw the traffic lights into a blinking confusion of red, yellow, and green that had caused traffic jams and thrown the city into chaos. Calls from the police and the fire department rang in every office at city hall.

Always the first person he would hear from was his boss McMurphy. "What the hell's going on, Kazem?" he would say. "You said it would work this time."

This made it the third time this month they'd had a problem. And each time they'd had to switch back to the old program.

He looked at the lines of computer codes:

```
If green = true
then
yellow = red = false
```

The ringing phone startled him. He didn't want to answer, anticipating that it was McMurphy. He was tired of being lectured to, tired of hearing that the system must be fixed, and soon. McMurphy would repeat the same old thing, that they couldn't afford to screw up again, that he was under pressure and they were in South Chicago, not some small, faraway place. That each minute hundreds of cars, buses, and trucks passed through the streets of the city, and if they failed, it would be the end of their jobs, the whole group would be sacked. Did he want that crazy old farmer to come around again?

The last time the installation went wrong, a farmer had driven his truck to the front of city hall. "Come on out, you all," he'd called out. "I have a present for you." Then he dumped his barrels of milk on the marble steps, yelling that he'd been stuck in traffic in 104-degree heat and all his milk had gone bad. From the windows of the lab they had watched the security guards and assorted office workers including McMurphy run out to try and stop him. McMurphy had just reached him when he slipped and lost his balance, going down on his back in a puddle of milk. But before the security guards could do anything, the farmer was in his truck and driving away.

The telephone rang again. Reluctantly, he picked up the receiver. "This needs to be resolved. Do you hear, Kazem? We can't afford to postpone any longer . . . Let me know what's going on before the end of the day." Then he hung up before Kazem could say anything.

An uneasy feeling took hold of Kazem and he asked himself why he didn't just pack his suitcase and leave. Then he wondered why, when he'd finished school, he hadn't gone back home. What was it that kept him from leaving? The chance of a better future and the relative ease of life here? The fear of the unknown and the struggle for a decent life back home? He couldn't say, and the more he thought about it, the more unclear it became, like the traffic lights that suddenly got confused and started to blink. He sat at the computer screen but was hearing his mother's voice the last time he'd talked to her.

"Kazem, my dear, what are you saying? What lights? Every time you call, you say you have to fix the lights . . . Are you well? Maybe it's better for you to go and be with your cousin Parviz. He's doing well, he has his own clinic. I'm sure he'd be happy to have you there. You remember him, don't you? When you were in high school, he was a university student and came to visit us." Kazem wanted to tell her he hardly knew Parviz, and didn't even know where he was. "Whatever you do," his mother went on, "try not to come back—the situation isn't getting any better. They're asking people to come back to help the country, but I don't trust them." Her voice had grown sadder and he could picture her in front of him, her eyes still warm but her face more wrinkled. As soon as he solved the lights problem, he would talk to McMurphy, he told her.

"Who's this Mash-Murphy?" she'd asked.

He had to laugh, enjoying her ability to lighten the moment—the idea that McMurphy had made the religious pilgrimage to Mash-had, the shrine of Imam Reza, and received the honorific title of Mashadi, to be known as Mash-Murphy.

The telephone rang again. "Hey, Kazem, McMurphy here. Just wanted to tell you, we only have till the end of next week. Get the guys to work on it even if you have to stay late and come in this weekend. You hear?"

"Yes, sir," he said. He put the phone down and sank into his chair. He looked at the flowchart with its circles and squares and mesh of interconnecting lines and the rulers, protractors, and bits of erasers like small gray worms scattered across it. Again he tried to review the logic of the flowchart:

If green = true
then
red = yellow = false
. . .

He changed the last line to left = right = true, made the same change in the code, and went to the maquette and turned it on, then watched the lights change from green to yellow and then to red. He was following the readout on the monitors when the lab door flew open and McMurphy walked in. His hair was combed carefully over his bald spot, but his reddish face looked puffed up and tired.

"I'm sorry," he said. "I didn't mean to be harsh. My director calls me into his office to chew me out every chance he gets." He waited and then stepped closer to the maquette.

"See how well they work? What the hell goes wrong at the intersections? I think it's a problem somewhere outside our system, some problem with the interface. Or maybe it's sabotage. Maybe someone doesn't want us to succeed. I have enemies here, you know."

Sabotage, Kazem thought. "Well," he said. "If it's something like that, we would need to get the right people involved."

McMurphy nodded, only speaking after a long silence. "I know this project is killing us all. Are you okay, Kazem? It looks like you're not really focused these days. You've designed and written code for projects bigger and more complicated than this. Is something the matter?"

He could see the lights reflected in McMurphy's eyes.

"I don't think it's just this project," McMurphy went on. "You seem preoccupied. What is it? Is your family all right back home?" He'd told Kazem he had an understanding of people who'd come to the US and left their family behind, and remembered how his grandparents missed the old country and talked about it all the time.

Kazem thought about the reoccurring nightmares he'd been having. In one he was in a familiar town in the foothills of the Kurdistan mountains, standing by a food vendor buying a sandwich. The sharp smell of mustard burned his nostrils. There were huge birds in the sky and fog, mustard colored and heavy, was descending. He couldn't breathe and in the confusion the sandwich fell from his hands. In the streets and alleys people were kneeling down and covering their faces. The birds kept coming, some flying very low, birds with shiny wings. Lights were flashing all around him and he kept looking at the computer screens, knowing that the birds were being controlled remotely and wanting to stop them. He had to do something. The computers were guiding the birds—he must stop them . . .

"Hey, man—Where are you? I was saying that we need to balance our lives, Kazem. We all have to. We have to find something to get rid of the work's pressure. I've picked up golf again. Weren't you playing soccer for a while with some of your compatriots? Do you still play?"

Kazem shook his head.

"We all need our distractions," McMurphy said, heading for the door.

Kazem turned to look at the lights, wondering whether it would ever work out for him to go back, and whether peace and democracy would ever return to his homeland. Just the other night he'd pulled his suitcase out from under the bed, the same suitcase that more than once over the last few years had been packed and then unpacked and pushed back under the bed. Often at times like that he would get on his bike and pedal as fast as he could on the bike paths through the city, feeling as if he were still a boy playing with his childhood toy—an old bicycle wheel he used as a hoop. He would run and drive the hoop ahead of him with a metal rod, the ringing of metal against metal in his ears. Behind him would be the other village boys, all with their hoops and happily out of touch with the world around them. They would run barefoot on the soft dirt of the alleys, going out of the village, through the cemetery, and down the narrow dirt road, the winter wheat green on either side, and then keep on toward the edge of town where they would buy lollipops and turn around for home.

The sound of blowing horns and sirens got his attention. He went to the window and saw a truck that looked like the farmer's speeding away with three police cars with flashing lights and sirens following.

He was still by the window when McMurphy raced in. He was breathing hard and his necktie was pulled askew as if someone had been trying to choke him. His thin hair was disheveled and his bald spot looked shiny.

"Did you see?" McMurphy said as he rushed to the window. "I knew it. I knew he'd be back. That crazy man. He just passed by the building. Did you see? They called me from the police station. They said he was driving through the city shooting at the traffic lights with his hunting rifle. And that he was heading this way."

McMurphy hit the maquette table hard with his fist. "I knew this project would be the end of me and now this terrorist farmer is after us."

Kazem stood, looking at McMurphy who went on saying that in this day and age, even in this country, one morning you would come to work and your boss would politely call you to his office and tell you you were no longer needed. Then it's you, your wife and children, your dog, your mortgage, your car payment. Then, as if he had remembered something, he hurried toward the door. But before leaving he turned back.

"Say, Kazem," he said, "you don't know that crazy farmer, do you?"

CHICLE UN CÓRDOBA

After attending to the last group of mothers and children who had come for their government handouts, he waved hasta luego to his coworkers and hurried through the crowded plaza to catch the five o'clock bus. The Plaza de España, in the heart of Managua, was abuzz with the calls of fruit vendors, shoeshine boys, and children selling chewing gum and candy. After three years of being in Managua, he still wasn't used to the crowd or the humidity. When the bus arrived, he struggled in with the swarm of people, holding his backpack tight against his chest. He knew the crowded bus was ideal for pickpockets.

As the bus haltingly started, he noticed the boy. He had soft light hair and was holding a box of chewing gum and calling out, "Chicle un córdoba, chicle un córdoba." In the confusion, no one was a buyer. All the passengers were holding tight to their belongings and trying not to lose their balance with the unexpected braking of the bus, but the boy kept on with his persistent high-pitched call. He'd seen many children like him in Managua, but the look in the honey-colored eyes of the boy touched him in some way. He took a coin out of his pocket and when the boy worked his way closer, bought a pack of gum. At the next stop a group of passengers pushed their way out of the bus. The boy was about to get off when someone knocked him, sending the packages of gum flying. He watched as the boy jumped off and began to search for the gum packages, and kept him in view until the bus turned the corner and the boy disappeared behind the ruined skeleton of a building, a memento of the 1972 earthquake.

At the Centroamerica stop, he got off, swung the backpack over his shoulder, and started for the nearby hills. He ran up the narrow half-mile trail, wending his way through the low trees and bushes, and arrived at the top sweaty and out of breath. He'd found the spot soon after he arrived in Managua and came often to get away from the oppressive heat of the city and the confined feeling of his workplace, always crowded with the widows, mothers, and children of the revolution who came to pick up bags of coffee, potatoes, or whatever was being handed out that day.

From the hill, the wounded city of Managua lay calm and green through the haze. He could make out the outline of the condemned cathedral—another casualty of the earthquake—and the stadium lights stretching up like four giant praying hands. Beyond, the lead-colored waters of Lake Managua extended toward the horizon, and Masaya Volcano loomed dark against the gray sky.

As the sun went down and the orange sunset spread out in front of him, a breeze began to blow and the noise of the city gave way to the singing of birds in the nearby bushes. He smoked a cigarette and thought of the city and the friends he'd left behind.

In those days they were full of hope for the future and any chance they got would head for the mountains. They'd camp overnight at the horse center and start to climb early the next morning. He wondered what the Shahpourians would have thought if they'd known that the university students they'd let camp there were young Marxists dreaming of the overthrow of the Shah's regime and everything associated with it, including polo and other bourgeois pursuits. He loved to see the horses when the stable workers took them out to run in the coolness of the morning, and often wondered if any of his comrades had been involved in putting fire to the stables.

They climbed for hours with their heavy backpacks. Sweat would run down his face, but the singing of his comrades was a distraction from the heat and the climb. When they reached the spring under the shade of the old oak tree, he would free himself from his backpack, pull off his boots, and run ahead, then splash handfuls of cool water onto his face until his shirt was soaked. Then they would sit atop the boulders and look down on the lemon orchards that stretched out on the bottom of the valley. Always he would think of Semira and wonder what she was doing somewhere down in the city.

Before darkness began to crawl up from the bottom of the hills, he got back on the trail and headed for the house where he rented a room. As usual, the old couple who owned the house were in the yard by the entrance, snoozing in their rocking chairs. What an amazing country we have, one of his Sandinista coworkers had said. "Our old folks with sad hearts nap in their rocking chairs, and our young men die in the jungle in the struggle for brighter days."

Carmen, her hair tied back in a ponytail, was busy with her three-year-old daughter, Rosa. Like him, they rented a room in the house. He greeted them with a buenas and tried to talk to the little girl. "Cómo estás, Rosita?" he said, but she lowered her eyes and hid behind her mother.

In his room, he switched on the fan, thinking it was lucky there was electricity. Then he took off his damp shirt, dropped down on the bed, and waited. Often when he was lying on his back in the small room with its bare cement walls, his eyes on the squeaking ceiling fan, his thoughts would circle . . . One, two, three, four—turn. One, two, three, four—turn . . . He was pacing his cell in the hellish summer heat to prove to himself that he was alive and would stay alive . . . One, two, three, four—one, two, three, four . . . He paced until he could hear the *shor-shor* of the cool mountain spring and imagine himself sitting with Semira next to him.

The rush of images would be interrupted when Carmen came into his room with a bottle of Flor de Caña and two glasses. Hola, she would say with a smile and then pull a chair up close to the bed. Returning her smile, he would straighten up, sit on the edge of the bed, and put his shirt back on.

107

Carmen would talk about her daughter and her day at the women's organization where she worked or about the Contra war and its casualties. She said very little about herself or her husband who had been killed by the Contras in the forests of Matagalpa.

Sometimes she reminded him of Semira. The way she tilted her head and looked at him. The way she tossed her hair to one side, and smiled. Or maybe it was the way sorrow nested in her brown eyes. He liked how they were able to communicate without saying very much. She told him she'd planned to study music, but then she met a young man who was a Sandinista and the revolution came. Now all she had was her four-year-old daughter and her work at the Sandinista Women's Center.

One night she came with the Flor de Caña and a book of poems by Neruda. She read a poem, her eyes sparkling and her ponytail swaying behind her.

Central America,
a land as slim as a whip,
hot as torture . . .

Nothing has really changed, she said after she finished reading, nothing—the same hopes and fears all around us.

In his halting Spanish he said he was glad to hear the poem in its original language and that the first poetry of Neruda's he'd read was the Persian translation of the Twenty Love Poems. He didn't say it had been a gift from Semira.

After a few glasses of Flor de Caña, Carmen said that Rosa had asked if he was her dad. No, mi amor, she'd told her, he's a friend who lives in the house like us.

They were quiet for a while, and then he tried to answer her question about how he had ended up in Managua. He told her about the revolution in Iran and being in prison and how young people like him had been used like a cheap piece of chicle that the boys sold in the plaza. He said he'd never imagined it would end the way it did. One day the door to his cell opened and a voice ordered, Put your blindfold on—let's go. The thought of another flogging made him shiver, but when they gave him a canvas bag with his belongings, he didn't know what to make of it. Soon he was outside the gate under the sharp rays of the midday sun. He had to shut his eyes, stretch out his hand along the wall, and kneel down until he got used to the bright daylight. Then he felt his shoulders shaking and realized he was crying.

He told her how, filled with hope and fear, he'd searched for Semira everywhere. He tried to talk to the people they'd known, but many weren't around. Some had gone to the Iran-Iraq War or been sent to prison for their beliefs. Some had run for their lives to other countries. And some didn't want to talk to him. But he couldn't give up. In prison it had been her love that had given him hope. They'd made a promise that if either one of them ended up in jail, they'd keep a low profile and never give up looking for the other.

Carmen listened intently.

Did she know, he asked her, what someone should keep in mind when being interrogated?

She shook her head.

They should always picture a bayonet held under their chin and say no to the interrogator's demands. In saying no, the chin moves up, but if it's yes, the chin moves down and then everything is lost and there'd be no end to their demands.

He went back to explaining about Semira. It was after months of looking, he said, that he found her name on the list of anti-revolutionaries who had been executed and buried in a mass grave under the dark of night.

Carmen reached out and took his hand.

From that day on, he said, he didn't trust anyone or anything and was constantly afraid of being taken back to jail or even executed. They often freed someone, then watched their activities and the people they visited so they could arrest people they suspected. He decided he had to leave the country. To get as far away as he could. He had some leftist comrades who were in touch with the Sandinistas—and may even have traveled to Nicaragua for training. With their help, he left the city that he loved, the city of lemon groves, for the icy winter of Moscow, where people in confused uprising were pulling down statues, then old Havana, with its proud revolutionary murals on every street corner, and then sleepy Managua.

He closed his eyes and images of mothers and children, the crowded plaza, and the boy crying Chicle un córdoba! flooded his consciousness . . . When he opened them, Carmen was sitting on the edge of the bed. He moved next to her, pulled her close, and kissed her. Then they stretched out on the bed. Slowly he grew calm, the thoughts and images fading away until all he was aware of was Carmen's soft breathing and the rhythmic movement of her chest going up and down and then the feeling of being on the mountain under the broad expanse of the sky.

KOH-I-NOOR

Ray had found the white Caspian pony on his latest scouting trip to Central Asia. She was like a jewel shining in the sun and he named her Koh-i-noor on the spot. When the pony arrived at the farm in southern Virginia, Liz was amazed at her beauty and loved the name Koh-i-noor. He explained that it came from the depths of history, when Nader Shah ruled Persia. Legend has it that on one of his incursions into India, the Shah was relaxing in his royal tent when an elderly maharajah was brought in. As the maharajah bowed before him, a brilliant stone hidden in his turban fell and rolled across the floor. The Shah, dazzled, grabbed the diamond and exclaimed, "Koh-i-noor"—mountain of light.

What Ray omitted in telling the story was that the maharajah told the Shah that if the stone was taken from its owner, the bearer would lose something even more precious and the stone would find its way back home. The Shah, disregarding the warning, took the diamond with him to Persia, not knowing that soon he would lose his mind and his empire would crumble. The diamond was lost and found its way back to India, destined to be part of the crown jewels of Britain.

Liz walked around the young horse, admiring her form and silver coat. She ran her palm over the pony's forehead and down the neck and withers, following the curve of her back. She listened to her breathing and, looking into the pony's eyes, sensed an uneasiness in them. She thought of mentioning it to Ray, but kept quiet.

111

Days later, the horse was behaving the same. "This is one awfully nervous pony," Liz said finally.

"She'll be all right," Ray said. "Give her time. She's come a long way and isn't used to her new home."

"I'm not so sure. Can't you see how she keeps her ears pinned back?"

Ray disagreed but Liz was insistent.

"Am I detecting a bit of jealousy?" Ray said only half-jokingly. "I could tell you stories from ancient times of a horse coming between a man and a woman."

"You certainly can't be serious," Liz responded. "Can't you see how uneasy she is? Can't you see the fear in her eyes when you approach her?"

Ray ignored Liz's concerns, and continued training the pony. He thought she was the most beautiful horse he had ever owned and had high hopes for her.

One spring day, sensing the energy and eagerness of the young horse, he rode to the edge of the meadow and let her go from a trot to a gallop. She raced down the path, her muscles quivering under his thighs and her hoofbeats echoing in his ears. He was thrilled by her speed and felt free, free from everything, from the past and the future, and urged her on toward the hills. But she suddenly veered down the valley and headed for a clump of trees, galloping as if racing against invisible horses where any attempt to control her meant go, fly. When he saw the forest drawing closer, he pulled hard on the reins, and let out a commanding *whoaaa, whoaaa,* but she wouldn't mind. Then he remembered how his brother had once stopped a frantic horse. He gripped the horn of the saddle, leaned down alongside the horse's neck, and reached toward her foaming mouth, wrapping his fingers around the bit and yanking it so hard that the horse skittered sharply to one side.

He couldn't have said what he heard at that moment—his scream, the shrieking of the horse, or the sound of the crash as he was thrown out of the saddle and against the white oak. It was dark by the time one of his stablemen found him half-conscious, his left thighbone smashed and his back badly hurt. Koh-i-noor, is she all right? was the first thing he wanted to know. But the horse was nowhere to be found. Everyone thought she must have been frightened and run into the woods. They searched the area for weeks, finding no trace of the horse.

Less than two years after the accident, Ray and Liz were forced to auction off their horses to pay their debts. They had expanded the stables on borrowed money and hadn't anticipated that the burst bubble of bad lending and the "toxic credits" the financiers were talking about would have such a drastic effect on their small horse center.

The house was silent after the bankruptcy. There were no horses or riders left on the farm, and no sound of nightly guests or chiming wineglasses. Everything was gone except for a few Persian carpets, along with some furniture and the two paintings of Koh-i-noor. And if it happened that you saw Ray in the hallway of the house, his white hair tied back in a ponytail, limping back and forth in front of the paintings of the horse, you might realize why, of all the paintings, only these two had been spared from the auction and were still hanging on the wall. One was a portrait showing the horse looking straight ahead, a forelock draping her forehead and her white mane cascading down her neck. In the other, she was running across the meadow, tail and mane flying, looking so alive you had the feeling that in the blink of an eye, she would gallop out of the frame and rush past you.

Liz was careful in speaking about the auction or mentioning their friends who seemed to have forgotten to drop in the way they used to. She would suggest a drive through the valley or going to a horse show, but Ray preferred to sit and talk about the time they met and the horses they'd known and trained. Her voice was calm and her pale blue eyes were as full of curiosity and radiance as when he met her years ago. She had come to the farm from *Horse World* magazine to interview a Persian immigrant attempting to breed Caspian horses. "The horse is nature's poetry in motion," he had said, trying to impress her, "a creature created by God to fly without wings." He explained that the Caspian was rediscovered in the northern part of Iran only a couple of decades earlier and, being a short horse with strong back and legs, was suitable for polo and jumping. He believed he was destined to make the Caspian a prize horse in the US, a dream that proved more difficult to realize than anticipated.

Ray often became impatient during the long afternoons. Looking out at the empty stables and training rings, and the meadows in the foothills of the Appalachian Mountains, he thought about the opportunity he'd had to make his home in this new world on land the first settlers cleared with their bare hands all those years ago.

One day, he suddenly jumped up from his chair. "Liz, did you hear that?"

"Hear what?"

"A horse."

"No, I didn't. I haven't heard a horse in months."

"If you would talk less and listen, you might."

"Ray," she said, "you're the one who's not listening. We should move away from here. We should have done it before all the financial problems."

"No," Ray said. "I won't lose my home again."

One afternoon, Ray came down to the hall and faced the bare wall where the paintings of Koh-i-noor had hung. He stood and stared until the outline of a horse started to take shape in front of him. First the muzzle, then the forehead, eyes, and ears, the neck and withers, and then the legs and tail. So engaged was he in the apparition that he thought he could hear the horse breathing. But when he reached out to her, a sharp pain ran through his bad leg. In the moment it took him to shift his weight, rub his aching thigh, and raise his eyes again, the image was gone.

He grabbed his umbrella and went out the door. Liz was on the porch reading, and when she saw him, she closed her book and looked up over the frame of her glasses.

"Why?" he said, banging the tip of the umbrella on the porch floor. "How could you?"

"My dear," she said calmly, "don't be upset."

"I am upset. I want to know why you did it."

"For your sake," she replied. "Every day it's something new. If you come to sit here for a minute, you hear a horse. You haven't mounted a horse for years, but you put on your riding outfit and pace up and down in front of the pictures, hitting the side of your boot with your riding crop. Why? So I would jump with each strike?"

"You couldn't even stand to see her picture on the wall."

"Don't start that again, please. You left me no choice."

"Choice!" he murmured. "How laughable."

He looked at her without saying anything.

"Are you at all aware of what's happening?" she said. "Do you realize I'm here and haven't disappeared with the horses?" Her voice trembled. "I loved our horses, too. All of them. Yes, they're gone. But you're here—I'm here."

"My dear," he said after a long reflection, "you've always been here. Always. We've gone through so much. But you shouldn't have taken the paintings down."

"I did it for your sake," she said again. "Koh-i-noor is gone, but you still can't let her go. I'm concerned, not just for you, for myself as well. We have nothing left here. We should move to town."

He pushed open the porch door.

"Where are you going?"

"Where am I going?" He pointed the umbrella toward the stables. "I'm going to take care of the horses. I'm going to see if a client is here. I'm going to call that good-for-nothing lawyer to see if he's come up with anything. I'm going to see what those lazy stable workers are doing."

"That's enough, Reza—enough drama for one day."

He waved her off and walked away, using the umbrella like a cane. Liz watched him for a moment, then took the days-old flowers from the vase and went to busy herself in the garden—a hobby she'd kept up with over the years. Now, with no horses to care for or boys and girls to give riding lessons to, it helped pass the time. From the garden she kept an eye on Ray, who had crossed the training ring and was over by the stables.

Ray stood at the iron gate and was about to push it open when he noticed the brownish spots on the railings. When he reached to touch them, oxidized pieces of paint and metal stuck to his fingers. He rubbed his hand against his pants. "How did this happen?" he murmured. "I need to paint this before it crumbles."

He hadn't been inside the stables since the day of the auction, but now, as if not in command of his will, he pushed open the gate. The hinges screeched and the sudden clattering of the mourning doves startled him. Through the dust dancing in the slanting beams of sun shining in from the narrow windows, he watched the doves settle on the rafters and start to coo.

The familiar smell of hay and horses drew him in. The first stall had been Koh-i-noor's. After the accident, he never opened it to another horse. He limped from stall to stall, remembering the morning of the auction. After stroking the forehead of each horse and pony—some that had won prizes for him—he'd kissed their foreheads and whispered goodbye. Not having the heart to see them being taken away, he'd left the farm with Liz. When they came back in the late afternoon, they found the place drowned in silence and the last rays of the sun vanishing over the red-tiled roof of the stables.

It wasn't the first time he had lost his horses. Thirty years earlier, in the wake of the Islamic Revolution that broke the back of monarchism in his homeland, religious zealots had attacked the horse center and burned down his barns. He and his brother, an officer in the army, had trained Caspian horses for the military and the Shah's polo club. Shortly after the revolution, his brother was accused of squandering the wealth of the nation and executed.

Over the years, he had tried to train himself not to dwell on the past, believing that a person driven from his homeland had to learn which memories to suppress and which ones to foster. But he could never fathom how it happened that, in those critical weeks before the fall of the Shah, he accepted an invitation to Saratoga Springs to give a talk about the Caspian horse, while his brother stayed and lost his life.

The old memories, like frightened horses, weren't calming down. In the stale air of the stables, he suddenly felt exhausted and hurried outside, gasping for air.

Liz waved at him from the garden. "It might rain," she called out. "Don't go too far."

"Okay," he answered unwillingly, and started down the trail that ran by the edge of the meadow. He stopped and examined the hoofprints in the baked mud, surprised that after months they still hadn't faded away, and tried in vain to see if he could match them with the horses. Then he poked at the sun-baked horse chips with the tip of the umbrella and watched them break into pieces.

He kept walking until he reached the hills. Then, rather than turning around and heading back home, he started down the valley. He knew where the tree was and wanted to see it again. He couldn't have said why and didn't gave it much thought. Where the valley flattened out, a wall of pines and oaks stood in his way, as if barring any stranger from the forest. Somewhere in the dark shade of the trees was the sound of running water and the smell of wet and dampness. A few more steps and there it was, the great trunk and the gap where the whitish wood was exposed like a bone in torn flesh. When he reached out to touch it, the tree felt warm as if it were still trying to heal its wound. He felt a tingling in his lame leg and pulled back his hand to rub the wrinkled lump on his thighbone.

His bad leg had fallen asleep. He bent his knee a few times to get the blood running. He could smell the damp and decay around him and felt a chill. He thought he saw shadows among the trees and then heard a sound from deep within the woods that wasn't any bird or animal that he knew, but more of a shriek. For a moment, he imagined it was a frightened horse. He took a few steps forward and listened. There was a dense rustling sound near his feet. A heap of ants swarmed on top of something dead. Shaken, he turned to go and saw the hill stretching up like a mountain in front of him. He hadn't thought about having to climb back up or whether his legs would carry him. Breathing hard, he pushed on and, after stopping to rest, made it to the top.

With the open field in front of him, he felt calmer and sat down to catch his breath. He thought about Liz, and regretted he upset her. Liz had loved and supported him through the years and helped him put what had happened in the old home country behind him and find a life here doing what he loved to do—train horses. He told himself that he had to let go of the bitterness of the bankruptcy and should go home to be with Liz and try to make it up to her.

The afternoon had turned gray and clouds had gathered over the mountains. The wind was starting to blow cold. He left the cover of the hills and started to hurry. It wasn't long before he heard the rain coming like galloping horses. Lightning flashed above the stables and thunder rolled across the field. He pushed on, half running, half walking, trying to keep the umbrella open above him, but it soon turned inside out. With a dry sound like twigs breaking, it was yanked from his grip. He watched the entangled mass of wet cloth and twisted metal roll on the ground and then be tossed up and down before flying down the valley.

Now he was drenched. His ponytail had come loose, and his hair blew across his face, making it hard to see. The path was turning to mud under his feet. He slipped and fell but pulled himself up and struggled on.

He could make out the house in the distance, but then there was something else—a whitish blur near the stables. It appeared for a moment and then was gone. Keeping his eyes on the path, he walked on. When he looked ahead, it was there again, a translucent form drifting past the stables. He was sure he heard the neighing of a horse and felt his heart jump.

"Koh-i-noor?" he called out. He could hardly hear his own voice. It was as if it were only a thought.

"I knew it!" he cried out. "She's back, Liz. Koh-i-noor is back! Don't scare her. I'm coming."

He walked on more urgently, not paying attention to the pain in his back and legs or the muddy path sucking up his last bit of energy. He lost his balance and went down on his knees. His arms and hands were shaking, but he managed to pull himself up again. Straining to see through the threads of rain, he could again make out a whitish-blue shape emerging from the mist like a whirlwind. It moved across the fields toward him and passed him with a terrible rapidity, leaving him with a curious sensation of lightness, as if he had been lifted up from the earth and carried away.

WHEN THE RAIN STOPS

He would never forget the words he heard in court. "Your honor," she said, "he's going to steal my children and take them back to Iran." Or the way she'd looked away, her voice pleading. And how he raised his voice before the interpreter had a chance to translate. "Dorogh migeh." The words had poured out of his mouth in Persian—she's lying.

He stopped walking, wondering how he would have stolen them. "My children," she had said, as if he weren't their father. And then the court took his passport.

He put up the hood of his raincoat and looked up the hill, the forest looked gray under the rain. He thought how every grain of dust that had covered them from the summer was being washed away. It had been six months, but he still couldn't believe everything that had happened. The changes took place so rapidly—first being separated from children, and then seeing them only once a week under the supervision of the state. Once a week.

Nothing has been this difficult, he thought, not even when he decided to uproot his family from their homeland three years earlier. His wife Soriaya was now his ex-wife—the sound of it so odd to his ears—and he had lost custody of his son and daughter. It had been almost two weeks since he had seen them because he'd missed the weekend before, and he was restricted from going close to the apartment.

The rain drummed on his coat as he walked. He went walking every day, an old habit from back home. Whenever he argued with Soriaya he would leave and wander in the park or go to a friend's and drink black-market vodka.

Were there signs he failed to see? Was there some way he could have controlled the rush of events? A loud clap of thunder echoed above the ridge. There are forces that sweep a nation, a culture, a way of life, he thought, and if you're in the way or are just working hard to take care of your family, they hit you hard. And if you don't break, you have to bend. In the old country, the revolutionary court almost took his life, just because he worked for people considered enemies of the revolution. And here, the court took his children away from him.

He missed his children and wondered how they were doing. He wished he could talk to them, to comfort them. He knew it was going to be hard to wait until his visitation time on Saturday morning. He hated the place the court had set up for their visit. He had to wait until the children came. And he couldn't go to them or speak with them in Persian, only in English.

A car passed and splashed the rainwater against his legs, but he kept on walking. I put up with so much nonsense, he thought, the way she kept pushing to leave the old country, always complaining that it wasn't a place for women anymore. Is it really any better here? And what should I have done? Let her run around naked? Woman, I told her, our way of life is different. You shouldn't go out wearing shorts or put on so much make-up or smile at strangers.

The problem, he thought, is that women like his wife don't know what to do with all the freedom. They get together and talk. "Oh, how could you put up with him?" one would say, and she then would answer her own question. "I wouldn't—I didn't. That's why I left him." And if they have American friends—some on their second, third, or even fourth husbands—they hear all about women's rights, and we see the result of all that. They find out that the law is on their side, that here children belong to their mothers, the opposite of back home. Then the lambs of the old country become lions in this one.

I did everything for my children so they would have a future, he told himself. I did so much for their sake, and hers. My house, my friends—I left everything behind. It wasn't my fault I lost my accounting job at the Shahpourian horse center when the family was accused of squandering the wealth of society. But all that is beside the point. We made it out of the country, and in court she accuses me of planning to steal the children and take them back home. And as if that wasn't enough, she says I'm always angry and scream at them. That I drink all the time. How could I defend myself through an interpreter? How can anyone trust these people—the judge, the lawyers, the interpreters? I'm sure they were playing with me. I think they arranged everything with that lawyer of hers. The same thing goes on everywhere. If I'd known that this country is run by women, if I'd known the language a little better, maybe things would have turned out differently. And that no-good lawyer of mine, he was only in it for the money.

Haven't I worked hard here? Haven't I tried to take care of them? Haven't I held down two jobs? Years of experience as an accountant and I have to work for the minimum wage at Walmart. We just needed a bit more time and things would have worked out. After the year in Turkey we made it here, and things were starting to get better. But no, she had to have everything right away. If we were back home I would throw her out like a dog, and my beautiful children would belong to me.

Another car sped by, a pickup, and he realized he was in the lane of traffic. He saw a woman and child sitting beside the driver. Suddenly a thought flashed through his mind. He stood for a moment looking toward the valley. What if he went back to Providence, got the kids, and drove away? He could go to another state, to some far place in this huge country. He fumbled with the car keys in his pocket. He still had the key to the apartment on his key ring. He wrapped his fingers around it and smiled. No one had thought of taking it away from him. He could picture his children sitting at the kitchen table eating breakfast and their mother, her back to them, washing dishes at the sink. He would park behind the building and use the back door.

He would do it, Soriaya thought, getting out the cereal box—he would take them back home, where no one could reach them. She put the bowls of Cheerios in front of the children. Afshin pushed his aside, but Mina started to eat right away. Since the morning, she'd had the feeling she needed to be patient with them, and with herself, and try to keep bad thoughts at bay.

"Afshin," she said. "Chera namikhori, azizam?"—Why don't you eat, my dear? She went back to washing dishes at the sink. Through the kitchen window, she watched the rainwater flow down the street carrying leaves and debris to the drain at the corner. She'd been extremely watchful since the day of the settlement. It had become her habit to look out the window for anything unusual.

She knew it was over, that there was no way back, and felt she had to watch the children more closely. But she wasn't sure about the days Afshin went to school and the afternoons she had to leave Mina at daycare and go to her part-time job at the mall. She'd heard on the news about children last seen by the school gate, and had often looked at the pictures of smiling children on the milk cartons. She'd even heard about children who had been taken out of the country. She glanced toward the children. I'll be fine, she told herself. We'll be fine. We'll survive, even if we have to pack and go somewhere else to start over again.

She watched the soap bubbles in the sink get larger and then burst. When a car stopped at the corner, she stiffened for a moment, then leaned forward over the sink to see better. A man wearing a raincoat got out and opened the trunk of the car, then took something out and got back inside. The brake lights went off and the car moved away. She turned to the children. "Afshin," she said, "if anybody knocks or rings the bell, don't open the door, do you hear? Let me know first, okay? Why don't you eat your breakfast?"

I have no regrets, she thought as she went back to her washing. I freed my children and myself. He'll never change. How many times did he promise to quit drinking, find a good job, not get upset with the children? Yes, it was hard for us to leave everything, family, friends. Yes, it cost us all we had. But we made it here, the place the whole world wants to come to. But then he started in on me. Why do you wear shorts? Why do you put on make-up? He wasn't like that in Iran, not that I could have worn shorts there. And then not wanting me to go to school. I always wanted to be a nurse. I didn't want to be a housewife at a young age like so many women. He promised that when we got married he wouldn't stop me from going to school. But it didn't work out because I became pregnant. And then his excuse was that we have two children who needed me. I could have managed, but he didn't want that . . . He didn't see it coming. He never guessed. I openly told him, Jamshid, nakon—don't. Baseh—it's enough. We're not in a country run by religious law. I'm a person here, not just a wife or mother. Don't put me in a cage. Let me be myself, let me have a peaceful place for our children. Wasn't that what we did everything for? Wasn't that why we spent all those months going from one consulate to the next?

Don't drink so much Jamshid, I begged him. It was my fault, he said. It was me who drove him to drink. Don't shout, Jamshid, I would say. But did he listen? I know it all started after he lost his job and ended up in so much trouble. But he took it out on me. At least back home I could have put on my chador and taken the children to my sister's until he calmed down. But here, where can I go, who can I turn to? The women I sometimes talk to, are they really my friends? Could I leave Mina with them for even an hour? Well it's over, and he got what he deserved.

"Maman," Afshin called.

"Yes, what is it?" She looked at the bowl of untouched cereal. "Chera namikhori?"—Why don't you eat?

"Nami kham"—I don't want it. He pushed away the bowl.

She stood beside him and stroked his black hair. "Chete azizm?"—What is it, my dear?

"I want to go to the park. Mikham football bazi konam"—I want to play soccer. "Now that Baabaa's gone, I don't get to play. I'm gonna go get my ball."

"In this rain? Maybe it will stop raining this afternoon. Then we'll all go. Now eat your breakfast. Be a good boy, azizam."

Afshin thought of the sunny summer days in the park playing soccer with his father. Mina would be on the swing with his mother pushing her. He loved soccer and wanted to be a goalie. He knew how to keep his eyes on the ball, dive with his arms and body stretched outward, and grab the ball and hold it to his chest, curving his body around it as if his life depended on it. He loved it and would look with pride on the occasional bruise on his knees or hands. Afterward, they all would go for hamburgers or ice cream.

The park was the one place his parents didn't fight. In the apartment, they were always screaming at each other. Sometimes he would take Mina to their room and try to play with her. But most of the time she wanted to be with their mother. And now his dad was gone and only called once a week, telling him to be a good boy, do his homework, be good to Mina. He'd promised he would come and see them soon and bring them presents.

Saturdays they had to go for a visit. There was a big room full of old toys. Sometimes there were other children. His father would be sitting on a bench and they would run to him. A woman would watch them and write things down. One time his father said something in Persian and she told him to speak only in English. They couldn't even go out for a hamburger or ice cream.

His mother came back to the table. "Chera namikhori?"—Why don't you eat? "Eat your breakfast. Look how Mina is finishing hers. She's only half your age, too. You're a big boy now—soon you'll be ten, and you know what? We're going to have a big birthday party."

"I don't want a birthday party. I want to go play soccer."

"We'll go when the rain stops. First to the park, then to Burger King. Basheh—Okay?"

Mina splashed milk and Cheerios all over the table. "Look what you did," her mother said as she fished pieces of cereal out of her hair. "Don't be a bad girl."

"I am not a bad girl," she screamed. "Khdat bady. Maman bady hasti"—You're bad. You're a bad mom.

She whimpered as her mother cleaned her face and smiled at her. "There," her mother said. "Beautiful again. My dear Mina. Now eat and don't make a mess."

126

Mina took the bowl from her mother and stared at her Cheerios. "A-tal, ma-tal to-to-leh," she sang. "Ga-ve hassan che-joreh." It was a Persian nursery song she sang with her father.

"Mommy," Mina asked. "Baabaa koo?"—Where's Daddy? It was a question she asked every morning. But today she kept asking. She thought about going to her parents' bedroom to see if he was still in bed. She wanted to sit on his chest and play with his mustache, then try to open his eyes. "Baabaa, Baabaa, cheshato va kon," she would say—Daddy, Daddy, open your eyes.

"Daddy's not home right now. Be a good girl, okay? Don't make a mess." Her mother finished cleaning the table and then went back to the sink and looked out the window.

"Maman, Baabaa koo?"—Mommy, where's Daddy?

Her mother ignored her and turned to Afshin. "Pesarakam"—My little boy. "Why don't you take your sister to your room and play with her until I finish cleaning up?"

Afshin got up and took Mina's hand.

"Let's go to the bedroom," Mina said. "Maybe Daddy is back."

SMILING PISTACHIOS

Frankfurt? . . . he says, knitting his brow and bringing his fingers to his temples.

Yes, Farzin says, thirty years ago we were in Frankfurt waiting for our visas.

He takes a pistachio and looks at it for a moment before splitting the shells with his thumbs. Then he drops the greenish nut in a bowl and adds the shells to the pile in front of him.

Frankfurt, he repeats and takes another pistachio.

Farzin remembers that Bijan advised him to listen to his father and answer his questions, but not to talk too much about the past because it tires him and makes him more confused. He suggested that they make tea, have some fruit, and play backgammon or cards—play Eleven, he said, he loves that.

But Farzin can't help going back to the past, not grasping how something that changed the direction of their lives could have vanished from the old man's memory. He wonders whether Mr. Rahimi has really forgotten or has decided to forget. But then thinks maybe it's the nature of memory to lose to the power of time. Farzin shows him the photos he took in Frankfurt. The old man points out himself and Bijan, but doesn't seem to recognize Farzin.

Che jaaleb, he says—how interesting. He looks at his younger self and then his son. Then he looks up at Farzin and back at the pictures. Shoma? he asks, pointing to Farzin in one of the photos. You?

Farzin nods.

How interesting, he says again. When was that? he asks.

Thirty years ago. We were in Frankfurt waiting for our visas to come to America.

Ah . . . Why?

We'd left Iran and were trying to come to America.

Yaadam nist—I don't remember, he says. He gathers the photos and looks at them again, taking his time, then piles them next to the pistachio shells and squares them with his thumbs and index fingers.

We left? he asks after a moment.

Yes, Farzin answers. There was a revolution and a war and many people tried to leave. We did too. I met you and Bijan in the pension in Frankfurt.

He listens without giving any acknowledgment. Behind him on the wall is a photo of him with his wife and children and grandchildren.

Do you remember the mother and two young children, Mr. Rahimi? She was trying to join her husband in Los Angeles and was always worried about her children. And how about that very dignified-looking man? People said he'd trained pilots in the Shah's military and was in hiding in Iran until Kurdish fighters smuggled him across the border into Turkey. And that if he hadn't escaped, he would have been executed by Sheikh Khalkhali—you know, "The Death Mullah." I still remember his name, Farzin says—Mr. Kochani. Funny how his name means someone who moves about. I wonder what became of him.

The old man looks at Farzin. Kochani? Che jaleb—how interesting.

Farzin, encouraged, says, How about when we used to go to the park near the pension, drink tea from a thermos, and talk about how lucky we were to have made it out of Iran? Mr. Kochani would recite poetry to us from Rumi and Hafez. But it was you, Farzin tells the old man, and your easygoing way and good humor that made everything bearable. Remember the mother and two children? You would play with the children, tell them stories and sing to them. There was one song about a fox. You would pretend to be the fox, holding your hands for ears, opening your eyes wide and looking all around as you sang. Farzin brings his hands up and tries to demonstrate but can't remember the words or the melody. It was for the children, he says, to calm them down, but we all listened and laughed.

The old man smiles.

The children would ask you to repeat it over and over again. "Dobareh, Aghay Rahimi"—Again, Mr. Rahimi—please. And you would, time after time.

But the world was different then, Mr. Rahimi. Nowadays, as you may have seen on TV, the world is in crisis and people, thousands of them, risk everything, climbing barbwire fences and daring the sea in tiny boats to find a safe place in some corner of the world.

We had it easy, Farzin says, looking out at the trees stretching themselves up to the third-floor windows. We took chances and worked hard. People helped us. It took a few years but we made it. I got involved in writing and journalism. You went into the building business. Bijan got his PhD and became a scientist.

Where's Bijan? the old man asks.

Don't you remember? He's taking your granddaughter to college. He'll be back tomorrow. He points to the note that Bijan left on the table for him. The old man picks it up and reads out loud. "Dad, as I told you this morning, Lila's school starts in a few days. I'm taking her to school. My friend Farzin will stay with you until I return. Don't worry, I'll be back tomorrow afternoon."

Farzin? the old man asks after he finishes reading.

Yes.

Oh, okay, he says and shells another pistachio. Then he gets up and walks into the kitchen, standing there as if looking for something. Farzin follows to see what he's up to. The kitchen smells of saffron and turmeric. Mr. Rahimi opens the fridge, pulls out several plastic containers of food, looks at them, and then puts them back. Then he examines the plastic bags on one of the shelves. They're filled with cracked corn and chopped lettuce. Each bag is labeled Friday. Farzin asks if he would like some of the chicken and rice that Bijan said they could warm up in the microwave.

He shakes his head.

It's quiet except for the ticking of the clock on the wall. The old man looks at the clock and then checks his watch, bringing it to his ear and listening to it for a moment.

It's slow, he says, taking off his watch and holding it out to Farzin. It's a Weston with a black-and-gold face and an adjustable band. The face is scratched and the band has lost its shine. Farzin pulls out the crown to reset it, remembering how they were fashionable in Iran in the old days.

My dad had a watch just like this, Farzin says. When I was little, he would come home for lunch and a short nap before going back. He would take his watch off and put it beside his pillow. I'd wait until he was asleep. Then I'd tiptoe over, take the watch and turn the crown, and stand fascinated by how the hands raced after each other and the calendar days flew forward in the little square.

I wish you'd met my dad, Farzin goes on. I'm sure you would have liked him. He was a chemist and worked at a petrochemical factory in Abadan. It was only a few days into the war when the Iraqis bombed the place. Many houses were destroyed, including ours. He did all he could to send me out of the country. He believed that my future was elsewhere. He too dreamed of coming to America, until old age and illness took his chance away. I miss the time I should have had with him.

Mr. Rahimi holds out his arm for Farzin to fasten the watchband around his wrist. Then he checks the time against the clock.

We had a house, he says.

It was in Tehran, wasn't it? Farzin asks.

The old man waits, looking out the window. The wind is sifting through the yellow and gold leaves. Would you like some tea? he asks.

No thanks, Farzin says, we just had tea.

Okay, he says, and they go back to the living room.

He holds out a pistachio to Farzin. Pesteh khandan, he says.

Yes, pesteh khandan—smiling pistachios. That's what we called them back in Iran, isn't it?

He nods, then shells the nut and adds it to the rest.

Where's Bijan? he asks again.

Don't you remember? Farzin says, pointing to the note on the table.

The old man reads the note again.

Farzin?

Yes.

You would come to our house, he says, you were Bijan's classmate.

I don't think so, Mr. Rahimi. It must have been someone else.

Farzin asks if he would like to play cards. He shakes his head and takes another nut. How about backgammon?

He glances at the board on the corner of the table and says, Do you know what's important in this game?

No, Farzin says. In truth, no.

He looks at Farzin as if to ask why he doesn't know. Ta-ajoobi nist—that's no surprise. Your generation doesn't take things seriously. He talks in a manner that Farzin wasn't expecting. From the first roll of the dice, you need to bluff. You boast to your opponent you'll block the rows on him, that you'll crush him, that you'll backgammon him. Then he loses confidence, you see. Then you try to close the Afshar row on him. You know the Afshar row? Farzin nods. And you try to close the sixth row on him as well—shish dar.

I see, Farzin says, khali khoob—very well.

It takes a clever player to jump over the closed sixth row, Mr. Rahimi concludes.

Right, Farzin says. Then, remembering how the Ayatollah Khomeini forbid playing chess and backgammon after the Islamic Revolution, Farzin asks, Well, should we play?

The old man stays quiet and Farzin's eyes move along with his to the trees behind the window. Would you like to go out? Farzin says, after a while. We could go to the park.

Before Farzin has a chance to think that Bijan hadn't suggested going out, the old man is on his feet. He heads for the bedroom and a moment later comes back with his hat and jacket on. He fills up his pocket with pistachios and gestures to Farzin to hold his pocket open. Then he puts in a handful of nuts and gives it a pat. That's that, the old man says as he walks to the fridge. Is it Friday? he asks.

Yes, Farzin answers.

Good, the old man says and takes one of the plastic bags of corn and chopped lettuce and hands it to Farzin. For our friends at the pond, he says.

Before they leave, he looks to see that all the lights are off, then shuts the door and checks the lock. As they get into the elevator, he starts to sing softly.

> The fox, the fox was sleek and gray,
> playing in the park all day

—That's it, Farzin says enthusiastically. That's the song—

> running here and running there
> enjoying the sun and chasing the hare
> but then the jackals came to town
> and chased her up and chased her down.
> And the fox, she kept on running
> until she found a hole,
> then jumping in quick as a flash
> she made the jackals howl.

Farzin wonders if the old man was using the poem to describe the situation in their homeland and he is only figuring it out now.

They get out of the elevator and Mr. Rahimi smiles broadly at a young couple who wave and wish him a good afternoon. "Good afternoon, dear friends," he replies.

Then he winks at Farzin and starts to hum the song as they go out of the building into the chill fall afternoon to see what awaits them in the park.

CONFERENCE OF
THE BIRDS

Fog like a fluid shroud covers the Public Garden. It's as if nothing else exists—no trees, no light poles, no sidewalks. The world reveals itself one step a time. Kochani would like to stay in the park and walks more slowly than is his usual habit. He stops every few steps and meditates on the bare branches that seem to emerge from nowhere, drops of water suspended beneath them like rows of teardrops. A fascinating phenomenon of nature, he thinks, this saturated air, this mist that doesn't transform itself into rain but instead wraps everything in its fluidity, haloing the lights and muffling the sounds of the city.

Kochani is on his way to his gathering. He leaves the park and crosses Arlington Street. When he turns and looks back, the park has vanished. Nothing is visible behind the curtain of fog.

Kochani never misses the monthly gathering held on the top floor of the building across the park. The day of the gathering he's often restless and arrives before anyone else. He doesn't know who named it Khaneh Ma—A House for Us All—or who "us all" are. He's certain he's never seen them at any gathering. Today he's early again. He goes in and slowly climbs the steps to the seventh

---

Kochani – One who wanders, migrates.

floor—Seventh Heaven, he likes to call it—and anxiously awaits the others.

Razi doesn't know that Kochani knows Razi has parked his car but forgotten to get out and is still sitting behind the wheel forgetting he's forgotten. Razi thinks he's at the Crossroads of Doubt listening to a white-bearded man in a greenish silk turban who must be the mystic poet Rumi ready to start his whirling dance, but then thinks, no, he must be Attar of Nishapur here for the Conference of the Birds. The wise man turns to him. "Strike the heart of doubt with your dagger," he says, but Razi, no matter how hard he tries, doesn't succeed in releasing the dagger from its sheath.

Yabandeh doesn't know that Kochani knows Yabandeh is on his way to pick up Jasmine but, not knowing which train station to go to, is trying to see the city from the air so he can locate the station. Jasmine, her long, disheveled hair growing wildly every second and spreading through the streets and alleys like a giant jasmine plant, is making Yabandeh so dizzy he knows it would be impossible to find her among the flowers. He raps on his drum in the hope of finding the rhythm of life, and thinks of the hermit Baba Kuhi sitting in his cave in the mountains above Shiraz, wondering what Baba Kuhi would do if he were in a busy T station in Boston.

He murmurs a jingle:

> Baba Kuhi, Baba Kuhi
> Tell me, Baba Kuhi
> What insights you have for me.
>
> Wasn't it you who said life's just a chore
> Oxen going round a millstone
> And not much more?

Razi – A Persian physician, mathematician, and philosopher (c. 854–925 CE).

Rumi – The Sufi mystic poet (1207–1273 CE).

Attar of Nishapur – A famous poet (1145–1220 CE).

Yabandeh – One who searches.

Baba Kuhi – A Sufi mystic from Shiraz (948–1073 CE).

Parastoo doesn't know that Kochani knows that after Parastoo finished entering her day's thoughts in her diary, the wind, finding her
light and agile, swept her off the steps of the Boston Public Library
and is carrying her to the "City of Kindly Friends" to start anew.

Rostamy doesn't know that Kochani knows that Rostamy, being
perplexed and compulsive, has forgotten to leave the monsters
from his nightmares at home and they've followed him to his car,
which is named Rakhsh after the legendary horse of the hero Rostam from *The Epic of Kings*. And that a few streets away, while he
was listening to one of Stephen King's horror stories, one of the
monsters had grabbed the wheel and another one had turned itself
into a truck and run into him so hard that he can't say exactly what
happened but knows that tonight he will encounter Stephen King
in a dream.

Ebrahim doesn't know that Kochani knows Ebrahim has taken
the book *Hilyat al-Muttaqin* and gone to the Red Sea to let Moses
know that if he crosses the sea, numerous unfavorable things will
be written about him and his people. The prophet is staring at the
sea intently and is so deep in thoughts of how he could help his
followers, who encircle him impatiently at the seashore, that he
doesn't see Ebrahim right beside him, and Ebrahim in vain pages
through the book of Muslim ethics trying to get his attention.

Sima doesn't know that Kochani knows that Sima has read the
story "Sunflower, the Forever-in-love Flower," by Shahrnush Parsipur, and that she, who is taller than any sunflower, had been on
her way to the House for Us All when she saw a pregnant woman
in the park and is taking her to a garden full of sunflowers to prove
to Shahrnush Parsipur that, contrary to what she'd written, the big
belly of a pregnant woman is more beautiful than a sunflower.

Parastoo – A feminine name meaning "swallow" (the bird).

Rostamy – Rostam, the hero from *The Epic of Kings* who fought the demons.

Hilyat al-Muttaqin – A book on Islamic morality by Muhammad Baqir
al-Majlisi (c. 1628–1699 CE).

Sima – "Beautiful visage."

Sar-khosh doesn't know that Kochani knows that on his way Sar-khosh has taken in the smile of an Indian woman, a red dot between her eyebrows, and lost his head, and his heart jumped out of his chest and started to dance Indian-style on the sidewalk, and when he had extended his hand to dance, his heart ran away in a flirting manner, giggling like the old khanzar-panzary man—the thrift-shop man in *The Blind Owl* by Sadegh Hedayat. So that Sar-khosh, put under a spell by the smile of the Indian woman, not only lost his heart, but found his temperature rising to the point that the snow and ice on the sidewalk started to melt, and now out of pure jealousy is heading for Sadegh Hedayat's crypt to call out to him from the hole in the wall and let him know that his Indian wife is on her way to the house of the old khanzar-panzary man.

Kochani, distressed and tired, goes to the window and sees Parastoo being taken away by the wind. She's tearing out the pages of her diary and giving them to the wind. She sees Kochani watching her and starts to recite the poem of Forough Farrokhzad entitled "Remember the Flight, for the Bird Is Mortal." When Kochani opens the window to step out and remember flying, the fragrance of tuberose and the sound of singing fill the room.

Kochani knows that Parsi is somewhere in a forest pouring his heart out, singing the song "Sweet Mariam" to ward off his loneliness. He tells himself it's a good day to go to the forest and walks away from the window and starts to circle the room. The more he circles, the more the desire of whirling and dissolving in time and place like a dervish awakens in him, but he knows that with the first spin he would throw up and fall flat on the floor. He goes back to the window, not knowing how to kill the loneliness. He wishes Razi would forget his forgotten-ness, get out of his car, and come and offer him his dagger. He knows that no one, none of those at the House for Us All, knows what he knows. They don't know he has witnessed the sparks of soul-shattering fear in the eyes of the most beautiful living creature on earth—the animal that he calls the poetry of nature.

Sar-khosh – "Happy-headed," name for an easygoing and pleasant person.

There's the sound of footsteps on the stairs. Someone is coming up. Kochani thinks it's the footsteps of Rodion Romanovich Raskolnikov, measured and purposeful—one . . . two . . . three . . . Thrilled, he listens more intently. But no, he knows those footsteps. It's Shivahi.

Shivahi doesn't know that Kochani knows the sound of Shivahi's footsteps, soft as the sound of water. He comes up the stairs and speaks calmly after taking a deep breath. "Mr. Kochani," he says, "why are you sitting alone? Come, come and see what's happening in town. What a sight to see." He's wearing dark glasses and approaches slowly, moving his white cane ahead of him. Kochani knows that Shivahi doesn't need his white cane because he sees everything with his heart. Shivahi takes Kochani by the hand and they descend the steps and leave the building.

The fog is still keeping the town hostage, and as Shivahi and Kochani walk on, they hear people saying that:

> Someone has killed loneliness with his dagger.
> Someone has found the rhythmic pulls of life.
> Someone has planted sunflowers all over town.
> Someone has driven all the monsters far away.
> Someone has started anew at the "City of Kindly Friends."
> Someone has learned to dance with his heart.
> Someone has learned to put out the fire of rage.
> And a bridge has been built over the Red Sea.

In the park, the fragrance of jasmine is in the air and someone is singing "Sweet Mariam." A bright smile comes to Kochani's face. He turns to Shivahi. "I must go, I must go. It's a good time to hear the woodpeckers in the forest." He hurries out of the park to go to the forest at Walden Pond, where he has heard that the drumming of woodpeckers echoing through the foggy forest is something not to be missed.

Shivahi – One who is lucid.

DARE THE SEA

"We're enemies" were his first words to Nazeer.

He was young, tall with a square face and wondering eyes. There were threads of white in his curly dark hair and a dull-reddish scar running from his chin down his neck. Nazeer remembered the first moment they stood facing each other—Nazeer wondering if he was Iranian and he probably thinking Nazeer was Iraqi.

He asked if Nazeer was from Iraq. "No," he answered, "I'm Iranian."

That was when he said they were enemies.

Nazeer hesitated. "That's possible," he said, "if we were on the other side of the earth. But we're here on this side and thousands of miles away. We can be friends if we want to." He held out his hand from behind the counter. "My name is Nazeer."

After a moment's silence he reached for Nazeer's hand. "I'm Samir," he said.

"Oshloon keifak?"

"You know Arabic?" he asked, surprised.

"No," Nazeer said. "But I'm from Khuzestan in southern Iran, not far from the border with Iraq, and there're many Arabs there." As soon as Nazeer mentioned Khuzestan, he saw the wonder in Samir's eyes intensify and felt his hand tremble. Samir released his hand, put a five-dollar bill down on the counter for the bread, cheese, and cucumbers, and left the store in a hurry. Nazeer watched him walk away beneath the palm trees throwing their shadows like spears over the sidewalk. He seemed to pay no attention to his surroundings and looked strong and proud as he vanished from view.

Every day just before sunset, Samir would come and buy something to eat and a pack of cigarettes and then walk to the beach. Sometimes after Nazeer was finished with work, he would take a couple of cans of soda and join him. Usually he would find him sitting alone on a bench in the shade, his eyes fixed on the sea and the sun. Nazeer would sit next to him and they would eat bread and cheese and talk.

On one of those occasions Samir gestured toward the people swimming and playing on the beach. "Look how carefree they are. Aren't they afraid? One thing that scares me is the sea."

"When I came here," Nazeer said, "I felt that way too."

Samir smiled. "Well, what is the sea to a person born in the desert? If it were a desert I wouldn't be afraid to walk into the center of it, right into its heart. But the sea, no. The place I set my foot must be solid."

The waves stretched back and forth by their feet. "We have a saying in Persian," Nazeer said. "The time comes when a person must dare the sea."

Samir fixed his eyes on Nazeer, as if to question what someone like him, living in Southern California, could possibly know about daring.

There was something about him, Nazeer thought. Maybe it was the mystery in his eyes or the way he didn't seemed to want to connect to anyone, but Nazeer still tried to see if they could be friends.

One late afternoon, Nazeer found Samir sitting in the usual spot and offered him a soda. "The sea is surprisingly calm today," Nazeer said. "And look at the sun—so huge, so red."

"Yes, looks like she's in a big hurry to go down," Samir replied.

Behind them, the palm leaves rustled as if in competition with the sound of the breaking waves. Samir looked out toward the horizon. "It reminds me of my village, Al-kabir," he said. "In my childhood days I wanted to know where the sun went at the end of the day. My grandfather used to say, 'It goes to the Red Sea at the end of the desert. She is tired from scattering fire all day and lowers herself into the sea to cool off.' Ever since those days I wanted to go to the Red Sea."

He was silent for a moment and then said, "It was the sun that saved me."

"Saved you?" Nazeer asked. "What do you mean?"

Samir stared at his feet and kicked the sand with his heel. "From that ancient burning desert, as you called it when we first met. From the world of stupid, crazy men. From people who won't leave you alone."

He lit a cigarette. "During the invasion of Kuwait and Saddam's dream of Greater Iraq, my platoon was sent to the border. For two months we were in the desert, in bunkers hidden underneath the sand. I heard they had fans, kitchens, and beds. What a lie! They were graves. It was like we had dug our own grave, twelve soldiers in each. Wherever you put your head or foot, someone else's head or foot was already there. Sand in your eyes, in your ears, your teeth, in the bottom of your throat. After a month, I couldn't take it anymore. One day, I crawled out and sat watching the sun shimmering at the end of the desert. It was just like the days we used to go out of the village with Grandfather. The Arabian peninsula was his entire world."

He stopped talking. When he was quiet and looked in the distance, it was as if he was somewhere miles away, in a place familiar only to him. He made Nazeer think about his own grandfather and his childhood days with him.

"That's our story," Nazeer said. "Having our heart in two places. We have to somehow keep our memories alive and find a way to feel at home here."

Samir suddenly got up and started walking. Nazeer followed him along the edge of the foaming surf. Then Samir stopped and turned. "I'll never get used to this place," he said. "This morning, at the 7-Eleven, do you know what the cashier said? He asked me where I was from, and when I answered, do you know what he said? He said I was the enemy. And then he asked who let me into this country. What can I say to that? You tell me."

Nazeer could see the scar on Samir's face quivering. He searched for something to say. He wanted to say that there were plenty of nice people around and that who knows, maybe this person talked to you that way because he had a friend or a relative or even a brother killed in the war, in Iraq or in Afghanistan. But he stopped himself. "It takes time," he said. "People like us, cut off from their home and in a new place, are sensitive to everything they see or hear. The bad things about our homeland seem better than the best things here, and at times the good things here become unbearable. Sometimes we get into a battle with ourselves which has no end. But the passing of time changes everything."

"Not for me," Samir said sharply. "I think it was a mistake. I shouldn't have come here."

"Well," Nazeer said, "I have an idea." He explained he'd been planning to move away. That he had a good friend, Parviz, who lived in Hawai'i. They'd been students at UC Davis and used to see each other a lot. His friend managed to finish school, but he had dropped out. His friend ran an animal clinic in Hawai'i and had been after him to move there. He could help them get jobs. Honolulu is very different from here, he went on, there are people there from all over the world. There are Iranians, Afghans, and he was sure Arabs as well.

Samir looked at Nazeer for a long time, as if he'd heard the most absurd thing. "I don't mean coming here, to California," he said. "I meant coming to the US. I wish I'd never stepped out of that desert grave, like many of my army friends. But I crawled out when we got hit. When the F-16s kept coming, with their horrible sound. Not one or two—the sky was full of them. In an instant the desert went up in flames. I remember the moment I was thrown into the air. Then, nothing. When I opened my eyes, I couldn't see a thing—I was surrounded by a circle of fire and smoke." He pushed his hands into the sand and watched the grains rain down between his fingers. "All I could think of was my older brother Taher. He was in the Iraqi army when the war started and Saddam ordered the attack on Khuzestan. After they sent his burned body back, my grandfather lived only two months."

Nazeer said he was sorry. He turned his eyes toward the horizon. The sounds of the sea gave way to the sound of artillery shells, of MIGs and sirens, and the cries of people. He tore off his clothes and plunged into the sea, swimming far out past the pounding waves. When he turned to swim back, he could see Samir, his outstretched arms disappearing and reappearing behind the cresting waves. He was beckoning to Nazeer. "Why did you do that?" he called out. "Are you crazy, going out that far?"

Nazeer wanted to say something, but no words came out of his mouth. "We had brothers and sisters too!" he blurted out. "We had homes too!" He realized he was shaking. Samir, stunned, stood staring at him and rubbing the scar on his neck.

Nazeer looked down at the sand. "I'm sorry," he said. "I don't know what came over me. These sorts of memories, as you yourself said, never go away."

Samir lit a cigarette, handed it to Nazeer, and lit another one for himself. They walked on in silence.

"For me," Samir said after some time, "there's no end to it. Like you when you didn't know what to do and ran into the sea, I couldn't figure out what to do. I was lost and confused. I started to run toward the sun at the end of the desert. She had a halo of dust around her. It was as if I saw my brother Taher there in the fire and smoke and I didn't want to end up like him. I don't know how, but I got out of that circle of fire. With my eyes fixed on the sun, I just kept on running." He gestured toward the horizon and the light reflecting on the surface of the water. "I still feel like I want to run toward the sun. Like in my childhood. In the evenings my grandfather and I would go out of Al-kabir—I'm not sure if anything is even left of our village. It's funny—the name means big, great, but in reality it's a very small place. Anyway, I would turn around and look at our shadows. I was fascinated with Grandfather's shadow. His mantle billowed out behind him and his shadow danced over the sand. We would walk and walk without ever reaching the sea. When the sun was finally gone, I would look around us and say, 'Abi, Abi, what happened to our shadows?' 'They've gone under the sand,' he would say. 'When the sun is gone, the shadows disappear under the sand.'"

Samir smiled and pointed toward the ground. "See, ours have gone under the sand too."

Nazeer looked at where their shadows had been. "Samir," he said, "tell me, after you escaped, what happened?"

"I kept running until it was dark," he said. "I didn't know how long or how far. Then suddenly there were bright lights all around me. They were American soldiers. Then I realized my clothes were scorched. The Americans took care of my burns and a week later transferred me to a Saudi camp. There were hundreds, maybe thousands of Iraqi soldiers there and every day more kept coming. I was there for about six months. We had to keep ourselves entertained. Everyone who had a talent would teach the others. We tried to learn some English so we could talk to the Red Crescent. It was a world full of outcast soldiers—soldiers who didn't dare to go back home. We were a headache for all the parties involved. If the Kuwaitis had gotten hold of us, they would have massacred us for sure, and the Saudis thought if they kept us under the sun for a few hours each day we'd melt into the desert sand. And after ten minutes standing motionless under the sun, you did feel like you were melting. The Americans didn't know what to do with us, either. Finally, the United Nations and the Red Crescent sent us to different countries. I came to the United States with a hundred other men. I was in New Jersey for three months and came here a month ago. It was my destiny to end up here, but in my heart I wanted to go somewhere else, someplace I chose myself."

Darkness fell over the ocean. Samir talked on and on. His words brought images of Khuzestan to Nazeer's mind. But he didn't want to bring up what the Iraqis did to his hometown and his homeland.

"Even with a million words I couldn't explain what happened in the desert," Samir went on. "How a person can age a hundred years in a day. Sometimes I dig inside myself, plunge deep into myself. Sometimes my insides become heavy and bitter, like this sea. I look at myself, think of myself, in Al-kabir, in school, in the military camp, here beside the sea. I ask, What happened? Where am I?"

After that evening, Nazeer would wait for Samir in the afternoon. When he finished work he would go to the beach and sit on the bench where they used to sit and talk. He would listen to the waves and watch the white lines of foam appear and disappear. But Samir didn't come.

Seven days later, on a Friday, Samir came into the shop looking happy and well dressed. He'd had a haircut, his short hair was combed back nicely, and his face was clean shaven.

"Where have you been, brother?" Nazeer said. "I'm happy to see you. You disappeared on me."

"I needed to be by myself for a few days," Samir said. "There was a war waging within me. As you said, the time comes when a person must dare the sea." He smiled.

He paid for the bread, cheese, and cigarettes, and Nazeer could see a sense of victory in his face. "The weather is beautiful today," Nazeer said. "When I'm done here, I'll join you at the beach. I'll bring a few bottles of beer to celebrate."

After work, Nazeer went to the beach. The weather had changed. The sky was dark and overcast. He didn't see Samir in the usual spot. He looked around, but the beach was empty. The sun, hazy behind a bank of low clouds, was sinking into the sea. When he sat down, he saw a bag a few yards away. It was the bread and cheese. They were untouched.

He followed the footsteps leading along the beach and his eyes fell on the Arabic words written in the sand. He knelt to read them just before they washed away.

Ana zehabt le altaqi ma el-Shams—I went to meet the sun.

NOWRUZ GIFTS

My dearest Parviz,

One of the hardest things in the world for a mother is not to have seen her son for years. This Nowruz, like many others, you're not here with us. For the coming of the New Year and arrival of spring we send you a package of gifts to help you celebrate the day that has marked our calendar for centuries.

The greens and the hyacinth were picked by me, your sister, and your grandpa from the open plains near our ancient sites. To welcome Nowruz, put them at the entrance of your house, and on the thirteenth day of the month of Farvardin, throw them in the running water of a spring to be taken back to nature.

The gray pouch contains a handful of soil scooped up from the four corners of our homeland and places we visited when you were a lad.

The red bag is filled with the flames of the Chahar-shanbe Soori, the *S* words that name the elements of the Haft-seen, the warmth of the coming spring, the sound of Amu Nowruz reciting stories, and the singing of musicians as they walk the streets and alleys welcoming the new year.

The golden sack holds the spears of the morning sun above the Zagros Mountains, and the purple one is filled with raisins and walnuts, honey and pistachios, and other sweets and nuts.

The small pouch is filled with traditional herbs and the sounds of families at the bazaar buying gifts for Nowruz in brightly lit shops.

The violet bag is filled with the breezes of the north, the bitter heat of the south, and the wind sweeping down from the snowy peaks of the western mountains and across the sand dunes of the east, along with the hoofbeats of horses and the dialects of the countless peoples who have ridden over the plains of this land.

The blue jar contains the water of the lakes and rivers and a small goldfish.

The scrolls are written with words of our poets—Omar Khayyám, Ferdowsi, Rumi, Hafez, and Sa'adi, not to mention Nima, Akhavaan, Shamlu, and Forough Farrokhzad.

The narrow strip of wood is from the crutch of a soldier returned from the front, the green headband is from a youth who stood in the city square and cried out, "Where is my vote?," and the small vial is filled with tears of the mothers gathered at the entrance of the prisons.

The yellow bag is filled with the cheery notes of the sparrows, the crowing of the roosters, the cheeping of the swallows, and the song of the nightingales.

Inside the rainbow-colored container are the cries of people at a soccer match, the laughter of schoolchildren released from their classes, the "hay hoy" of a dervish in the bazaar, verses from *The Epic of Kings* being recited in the teahouses, the scent of mint and tea, and the smell of fresh bread.

In the saddlebag you'll find the colors of the traditional clothing, the designs woven into the carpets and kalims, and the geometric patterns of turquoise tiles, along with the music of the tar and the saz, the singing of the shepherds, and the cry of newborn lambs and baby goats.

The blue sack is filled with the color of the sky, the sparks of the desert stars, and the sadness of those who are refugees in their own land.

In the small green jar are patches of white clouds, droplets of rain, the sound of growing grass, and the soothing coolness of the breeze over the wheat fields.

In the perfume jar is essence from the lemon trees of Shiraz, and the silver bowl is full of Shirazi Falodeh to divide among your friends.

In the large shiny bag are knowledge and faculty, honesty and loyalty, courage and dignity, friendship and kindness, hope and desire, forgiveness and generosity, peacefulness and pleasantness, along with the advice of the prophet Zoroaster to practice Good Thoughts, Good Words, and Good Deeds. Open the sack and let them spread to the wind that they may travel wherever humans have settled.

There is another bag I need to tell you something about, you must keep it fastened and bury it in a faraway place because it holds ignorance and incompetence, cruelty and wickedness, animosity and ugliness, curses and anger, lies and grudges, pessimism and stubbornness. We only send them to let you know that in this land of ours we are still battling these difficulties.

My dear one, as you know, the gifts from all corners of this ancient land are numerous. We may unwittingly have missed many of them that we can only hope to send next year. These are only a few things to show people where you live so they know how Nowruz has been celebrated over the millennia and that we have always welcomed spring and the New Year with the hope that light will win over darkness.

> Hameh ruz-at Nowruz baad—
> May your every day be a Nowruz day.

Come back for a visit. I'm waiting, my eyes are on the road.

Love,
Your mother

FORTY DEGREES

My dear friend Parviz, you were lucky to get out of this city, and luckier than any of us to get out of the country. And not just that, to go as far as Honolulu, and to find out that you dropped the idea of having a family practice and became a veterinarian—bravo, what a bold move. I can't remember when I had any news from you, was it a year ago, two years ago, maybe more? Can't really say. Too much confusion these days. And did you say that you were planning on a trip back home? I can't imagine what for, have you lost your mind? But if you ever do come, please look up your old friend Layla, and come by the hospital, given that I'm still around. As you know, this old country of ours is full of surprises and unpredictability.

I'm afraid I may trouble you with these words, but there's something I need to tell you. I hope what I'm about to say I haven't already said. Maybe I have. I don't know—what confusion. As far as I can remember, I haven't told anyone, but no one is left—I mean none of those people we used to know or went to medical school with or even our colleagues at the hospital—they've all taken different directions in their lives or been driven away. Anyway, I must have written you about those sorts of things before. And now, you may be asking, What does she want to tell me this time all the way from a country I left behind years ago? But please, be a good man and read. I want to tell you about the elementary schoolgirls I've been studying and what I've seen at the school's sports hall—I guess in America you call it a gym.

Believe me, this study has brought me sleepless nights. Even if I'm lucky enough to fall asleep for a short time out of sheer exhaustion, I have bad dreams. The same dead-end dreams, the same struggle to reach the door of the gym to find out what is going on. Then I suddenly jump awake with the shouts of the principal who doesn't let me in. She's always in my dream, and then lost between dreaming and waking I can't get rid of my fear for the little girls.

Oh, God, what am I saying? . . . Forgive me. I wanted to tell you about the project. It's similar to the UNICEF study we did years ago when we were pre-med students—the body temperature, heart rate, height, and their correlation with age. You must remember, it was a simple project and we reported to Dr. Saffarian, the head of the children's wing of the hospital. You asked me to choose the school and we went to Meher Primary School in the old part of Tehran. It was the school I attended. You were disturbed to see such a poor school compared to the one you went to.

In the last couple of months, I've been visiting the girls at Meher School—I mean Zahra, the name has been changed to a religious one—and the hijab doesn't come off the little girls even within the four walls of the school courtyard and in the dazzling heat of the day. There was something else . . . Oh, Lord, what was it I wanted to tell you? . . . I've become very absent-minded these days—I don't even know when it all started. You see, right now I forgot what I was going to tell you. It's not only me, mind you, everyone living in this old city of ours is in the same situation. Take the way we move our things around inside our own homes as if carrying out a ritual. We move whatever belongings we have, dragging them from one room to another—furniture, books, dishes, clothes. You can hear this awful, constant slow screeching of things being pulled across floors all over the city, especially at night. We clean the house, dust, wash, pray and do blessings, pastimes that distract us from reality. It's an epidemic, if you ask me.

A while ago, when I, too, was moving things around in my apartment, I came across my old research files for the primary school project. As I leafed through the pages, I could see the little girls in front of my eyes. They were standing in line waiting to be examined—do you remember how excited they were, running around in their school skirts, their hair let down, playing and singing? I can still hear them reciting the old nursery rhymes we knew so well . . . How did it go . . . I used to know it . . . Oh, yes, it went something like, Atal, matal, tootoole . . . gov-e Hassan chejor-eh . . . Well, I don't hear this song anymore. Singing and dancing are prohibited these days. What memories . . . the days of medical school, and our dreams and bright future. Well, let it be . . . let it be.

Anyway, looking through the files, the idea occurred to me. Why not go back to the same school and repeat the study? Years have passed and a few generations have come along. I thought it would be an interesting research project and was lucky to be given permission by the Department of Health Ministry to go to Meher School—I mean Zahra, that's the new name. Anyway, every week whenever I found a bit of time, I went over to the school and examined the girls. Now I'm disturbed and confused by the results. It's strange. The girls' pulse is above normal and their temperature is high—almost 40 degrees. They're all running a fever. You probably don't believe it or think I've made a mistake. I assure you it's neither a mistake nor my imagination. You used to tease me, remember? When I came up with an idea, you would laugh and say, "Oh, what an imagination you have, Layla." Well, this isn't my imagination. It's real. With the little time I had and all the difficulties the school principal made for me, I managed to repeat the tests three times.

Years ago, when we did the research together, everything was normal. You must remember discussing our results with Dr. Saffarian. "My dearsssssss . . . my dearssssss," he used to say, waving his hands in the air, "the essential thing is oxygen, oxyyyyyyygennnnn . . . The heartbeat, the body temperature, all depend on oxygen getting to the brain." He would tap his bald head with the tip of his finger. "If there is lack of oxygen, the brain is doomed. Try to understand."

At first we thought he was joking. It took us a while to figure out that he was talking about freedom.

Poor Dr. Saffarian! I think he, being a member of the generation that had lost so much in the social unrest, felt he had to warn us not to make the same mistakes. Ah, did you know what happened to him? Maybe I wrote to you about it. It was a year ago—or was it two? I saw him in the hospital hallway. He was smiling and commenting on the beautiful morning, although it was gray and thunder rattled the windows. By afternoon he had taken off all his clothes and danced nude through the hospital halls and down the stairs into the yard and out to the street and under the cold driving rain. Can you believe that, dancing naked in the streets of a city where dancing is forbidden?

There's no trace of him and I miss him terribly. He was a brave man who in his own way tried to tell us something. What if all of us in this city of ten million were to take off our clothes, hijabs and all, and dance through the streets? Do you think the moral police could control a dance uprising? It's occurred to me many times to do what he did . . . At any rate, who knows, maybe one day you will receive a note or a phone call from him, telling you that he is not just in America, but in your town or even in your neighborhood and has found a job at a hospital. But if you ask me I would say he has not been able or allowed to go beyond the perimeter of this city.

Oh, God . . . My dear Parviz, why am I telling this to you all the way on other side of the world? I wanted to tell you about the schoolgirls and the exercises they do in the gym. One day I tried to see, but as soon as I got to the gym door, the gloomy principal appeared from nowhere. "What are you doing?" she shouted. "You're not supposed to go in there."

I became so concerned for the girls that a few days later, I left the hospital in the middle of my shift. You can't believe how busy and overworked we are these days, taking care of suffering people, not just from physical maladies but from anxiety and fatigue. Many times they just want someone to listen to them talk about their lives. Men and women, old and young, even children—they all come to us, as if we're any better off than they are. Ah, I remember, you said you gave up medicine and became a veterinarian to take care of little animals, I could very well relate to that . . . Anyway, I was so keyed up that I left for the school. The sun was unbelievably high and bright and my skin was burning under the dark, heavy hijab. My heart started to race like I was running a fever. While I stood at the street corner, feeling dizzy and waiting to cross, I don't know why, perhaps because of the brightness of the sun, I was mesmerized by the blue and turquoise colors of the minarets on the other side of the square. They seemed to be fountaining up into the hazy sky when suddenly the gesturing of women rushing by compelled me to get out of there fast. As if awaking from a dream, I saw two hijab police in the shade of the minarets. A bearded policeman and a policewoman in full hijab. They were arresting a young woman for wearing lipstick and letting a strand of her hair out from under her scarf. Terrified, I quickly ran the back of my hand over my lips to get rid of any lipstick even though I knew I wasn't wearing any, tightened my scarf over my head, and rushed away.

When I got to school, it happened to be sports period. To my surprise no one was at the door, so I went in. All the girls were standing in line in the old, dark gym with cement walls and floor and narrow, tightly curtained windows. The girls were listening to the principal. She's an ordinary-looking woman but lets you know she is in control and has an agenda. She ordered the girls to put on this outfit. You should have seen it—two big wings strapped to their arms. Imagine that, in the midday heat with no air conditioning in the old building and only ceiling fans turning slowly. From the look in their eyes I could see they were aware of what awaited them. Then with the blast of marching music—or was it the music from a passion play?—they started to flap their wings. The principal was calling out, "Faster, faster my angels. Fly to heaven." I stood there absorbed in the scene when suddenly I was startled by the principal shouting at me. "What are you looking at? Get out of here right now!"

My heart is heavy for the schoolgirls and I don't know what to do or who turn to. No one would listen to a thing like this. I can't sleep anymore. Sleep, the state that is supposed to help sustain us in this world and shield us from reality of it, has lost its function for me. And if I fall asleep, I see the girls in that heat flapping their wings, their faces covered with droplets of sweat, just the same way I see them in the gym.

One day when I was examining the girls with the principal standing by, a young woman, the mother of one of the girls, came in. Their conversation soon escalated into an argument about the bruises on her daughter's arms. I can't say for sure if this was in my dream or really happened. I can't differentiate anymore. I'll tell you this, though. It seems to me that all of us in this city are in the same situation, we can't differentiate between the real world and our dreams. I see it in people's eyes—my coworkers at the hospital, the baker, the butcher at the neighborhood market, the people on the bus. We're confusing the dream world and the real world, witnessing certain things during the day and then seeing them again in our dreams and nightmares.

I'm restless and worried. No, not just worried, afraid. Every day the anxiety heightens. It's like not knowing who you are anymore, what your aim in life is. You dig within yourself to figure out what to do in this place where the boundary between life and death is thinner than a razor blade.

Forgive me. I'm afraid I've troubled you. I got carried away and forgot my main purpose in writing to you. The main purpose . . . What was it? . . . Oh, yes. The health of the schoolgirls, their heart rates and temperature. It is strange. These little angels are burning with a constant fever.

I wish you were here and I could talk to you in person. Do you remember how we used to talk about the future? It was your destiny to go away. No, I shouldn't say destiny. Maybe it's all in our own hands. Going away—is there really such a thing as going away? These days everyone talks about going away, going anywhere things are better. Strangers in a taxi or in a bus turn to you and ask if you know a way to leave. Don't they think that if you knew a way out you wouldn't be sitting there? The authorities are constantly bombarding us with their view that those who have left the country are wilting away in foreign lands like uprooted trees. But no one says that even in our own land, the way branches are being broken and leaves ripped down, no matter how strong or deep the roots, the tree will die. Don't they realize that leaves are the lungs of a tree and the way of getting oxygen to the roots? Poor Dr. Saffarian was right, saying. "It's all about oxyyyyyyygennnnn . . ."

At times like this or at night when I wake up from my dreams gasping for air, I think about you. I try to imagine you in America, and of all places in Hawai'i—"Paradise on Earth," isn't it what they call it? It must be nice to work there, to attend lectures, to do research and publish your results. We have lectures and talks here, too, as much as one's heart desires. We are bombarded with talk—from the radio, from TV and the newspapers, and from loudspeakers throughout the city, filling up our ears with talk of progress and plans for the future, plans to manage not just our society but the world, since it's gone astray and only they know how to save it.

Anyway, you left. An opportunity presented itself and you managed to leave and go as far as you could to the middle of the Pacific—amazing! As you very well know, in this land of ours, the doors have always been more open for men. For us women, they've been kept closed, although I believe with all my being that it won't last. But for now, even the door to the gym is shut hard in my face. I can still see the girls with their white wings strapped to their arms. They're standing listening to the principal tell them about their place on earth, that they will grow up to become good wives and give birth to many children. The music is blaring and the girls are flapping their wings. Standing on their toes, they jump up to leave the ground, then exhausted and out of breath, they fall down one by one, their mouths half-open, gasping for air like heat-stricken birds.

I've witnessed all this. I've seen it in my dreams. And I know it'll be the same tonight, tomorrow night, and the next night. Last night I saw myself amid the girls. In our white angel uniforms, we were holding hands and going around and around the gym, dancing, laughing, and singing, when suddenly flames rose from the curtains and in a second the place was ablaze. In a burst of smoke and flames and to the blare of trumpets we flapped our wings and soon one after another were in the air, rising above the burning gym, the school and the park, and then the blue minarets and domes of the city.

MAGIC ISLAND

Swaying and wobbling, feeling like a circus clown trying to keep his balance, Parviz continues on his way. He isn't drunk but wishes he were. He wishes he'd had a few more glasses of the mijiu wine that Mrs. Yung put on the dinner table. Maybe it's jet lag that's clouding his mind. He thinks he shouldn't have listened to his messages. First it was his father, yelling into the answering machine from the other side of the earth. I sent you to America to become a doctor, he bellowed out in all his fatherly authority, and you become a dog doctor! A Muslim and dog doctor! And you dare to come back here? What for, to shame me? Stay in America with your cats and dogs and don't dream of coming back here again. He couldn't even wait until Parviz was back and must have called him while he was midair. Next was Mrs. Yung's message. Dear Doctor, she said, cheerful as usual. Welcome back to Honolulu, I hope you had a good trip back to your home country and have returned safely. Come have dinner with us. We would love to see you and hear about your adventures. I'm just back from China. I was there for the New Year. Xin nian kuai le—Happy New Year. It's the Year of the Dog.

Why did he accept her invitation? It would have been better if he'd stayed within the four walls of his bedroom and lain in the dark. And that's just what he'll do if he ever finds his way home. What an evening it was and how they talked. She of going home after forty years and he after ten. She of Tiananmen Square and how beautiful it was and he of Freedom Plaza and how gloomy. She of the students in front of tanks demanding freedom and he of people marching and calling out, Where is my vote? She of Beijing streets packed with people bicycling and he of the dusty city of his ancestors on the edge of the desert, crowded with traffic and morality squads. And she of her father who years ago had spent all he had to send her to America and he of his father who'd been unhappy with him from the moment he set foot back in his childhood home. They went on and on, her ancient-looking husband sitting in his wheelchair, watching all the while.

Yes, what a wonderful trip it was, Parviz tells himself, and what a welcome he received. How foolish of him to think it would be a trip of reconciliation. What a glorious visit to the glorious old country after all those years.

Why didn't he listen and let Mrs. Yung call him a taxi? Instead he left on foot, thinking the fresh air would do him good.

The streets are empty and a light rain is starting. If it were daytime, a rainbow would certainly be popping up over Manoa Valley to wash itself in the gentle rain before fading away. An ambulance shrieks through the intersection, followed by a flashing police car. Parviz stops and covers his ears until they've passed. On the terrace of an apartment, the silhouettes of a couple appear and a woman's laugh rises over the soft jazz.

He lingers in front of the Aloha Lounge, fighting the temptation to go in. Then he recognizes the man coming down the street, a lanky man in a white tuxedo carrying a briefcase. Handcuffs, one cuff around the handle of the briefcase and the other around his wrist, gleam metallically under the streetlight. Parviz has seen him before, reading in the Kaimuki Public Library and walking the streets. Just recently he learned from a client of his, an older gentleman who always brings news of the neighborhood, that this haole man was homeless and new to Honolulu. And that when he was picked up by the police on Magic Island soon after he appeared on the scene, he had quietly protested, saying, Peace is every child's birthright. And do you know, his client asked, what they found in his briefcase after they managed to take the handcuffs off? Parviz shook his head. A Bible and an American flag. Parviz couldn't totally get his meaning, but his client chuckled and went on. Doctor, he said, tapping his temple with his index finger and winking, Magic Island attracts all sorts of people—special people, if you know what I mean. Parviz smiled and started to examine the old Akita, his thoughts drifting to Magic Island and the young woman he met there. *I'd like to go under the magic sea*, she sang softly, *to where the sea god sleeps. When he wakes up, the islands weep* . . . She had the ocean in her eyes and the little silver bells around her ankles jingled as they walked along at the edge of the surf. They sat together and watched the sun sink and the evening darken the ocean. She shared her tangerines with him and he shared his chocolate bar with her. He opened his eyes to the sound of jingling and found her gone.

Parviz watches the man with the white tuxedo and briefcase approach. He thought of befriending him and now for a second thinks he should seize the moment. And when would be better than this fantastic night? Parviz greets him with an aloha, but the man passes without raising his head or giving him a glance. He seems to be in a hurry. Maybe he's heading for Magic Island. Maybe he's going to see the white horses a man once wanted Parviz to see. Look over there, he'd said, pointing beyond the waves. Look there, look at the white horses. See how beautiful they are, how carefree, how they trot. See their manes and tails against the blue sky. The man was youngish, sunburned and shirtless. We're all in an ecstatic dance with nature here, he said, and it may well be the last dance. Then he dashed away, his ponytail bouncing against his bare back.

Parviz continues on his way, but where is he? He doubts if he's on the right street. He should be in his neighborhood by now. He stands in the middle of the sidewalk, under the shadows cast by the palm leaves, and lets the soft rain fall over him. The smell of earth and rain in the air is very familiar. In their desert town, it would rain unexpectedly, the alleys seeping with mud. He tilts his head back, his eyes closed, and feels the soft rain drizzle on his face. He can hear his father across the years, yelling, What's with you standing in the rain? Not paying attention and just to annoy him, Parviz would stand in the middle of the yard, his face held up to the sky until his hair was drenched and water dripped down his neck. Something isn't right with you, his father would shout. I swear to Allah, something isn't right. Only crazy people stand in the rain. Then he would reach for his belt. Parviz and his mother would run out of the house, into the alley slippery with mud. Mother, please, we should get away, we should go to Grandfather's, to that little desert town.

Three slim young women in flip-flops, yoga mats under their arms, look his way and giggle as they walk to their parked car. He brushes the rain from his face and starts to walk again. In front of the Kim Chee Restaurant, he quickens his pace to get away from the smell of Korean barbecue. It reminds him of the dish with the salty taste and sharp smell that Mrs. Yung served. To Parviz's surprise, she hadn't invited any of her usual guests, the people from the East-West Center, the downtown lawyers and bankers, or the friends from the garden club who formed her circle of acquaintances. He would have liked to have seen the retired professor of Eastern religions. That frail, soft-spoken man would have put him at ease with his calming voice and one of the mythological tales he liked to tell. One evening when they were sitting in Mrs. Yung's living room drinking green tea, the professor had patted Chochai's head and asked Parviz how much he really knew about the animals he took care of. Did he know, for instance, that at the dawn of existence it was the dog who lost us humans the chance of living for eternity? And that they'd been trying to make it up to us ever since by being loyal and obedient? He couldn't remember, he went on, which of the hundreds of gods it was who decided to send a dog with the message that humans should sprinkle earth over their dead so they would regain their lives. But on his way the dog got into a fight with a cat, so the god sent a sheep. The sheep came into a lush green garden like this paradise of ours and took her own sweet time grazing in a pasture. Then, not remembering the message clearly, she told the humans that the god wanted them to bury their dead. That's how it got all screwed up, you see, and he for one was very happy it did. Very happy indeed. Eternal life! What a mess that would be—imagine!

Parviz would also have enjoyed seeing the gentleman with the white goatee and thick glasses who always told stories about Christians In Action. Get it? he would say, that's what they called the CIA in the days of the Soviet Union and China under Mao. Parviz never knew whether the things the old man talked about really happened. Like the story of being poisoned in a Moscow hotel room—food poisoning, you know, he said, smiling at Parviz, one of their old tricks—and being taken to the hospital where all they brought him to eat for a week, every breakfast, lunch, and dinner, was a bowl of alphabet soup. He wouldn't eat even a spoonful because when he stirred the watery soup the letters would come together and form suspicious questions. The old man was sure that if he'd eaten the soup, he would have murmured the answers to the interrogation questions. Ha, ha, ha—he laughed his usual dry laugh—they thought they were being clever and were going to outsmart me. By golly, I showed them. I ate only the crackers.

But tonight Parviz was the lone guest and listened as Mrs. Yung pushed dishes his way, saying, Oh, Doctor, you should have some of this, some of that, and talking in detail about the taste, color, and texture of the things she'd eaten in Beijing. She said she had dishes—here she leaned forward as if whispering a secret—dishes that wouldn't be allowed in this country. You know, she said with a knowing look in her eyes. Parviz stopped chewing and looked at her dog, Chochai, who was sitting by the leg of the table, wagging her tail and looking at him expectantly.

It was one early morning about two years ago that Mrs. Yung had showed up at Parviz's clinic with the little Pekingese in her arms. He thought she looks just the same—well dressed, round-faced, pearls at her ears and neck, still proudly showing her beauty. The way she wore her hair gathered in a ball with two hair sticks stuck through made her look like she'd just stepped out of a classical Chinese painting. Mrs. Yung said the little dog had appeared in her garden from nowhere about a week after her old dog Chochai died. When Parviz took the dog, her round eyes darting back and forth, and put her on the examining table, a violent trembling ran through her body. At first he thought it was the odor of drugs and alcohol in the clinic, but the dog was underweight and bruised and it was clear she'd been kicked and beaten. When he told Mrs. Yung that he couldn't find anything wrong with Chochai, the old woman's eyes brightened and she put her hand on Parviz's, happy he called the dog by her old dog's name. It must have been destiny, she said, that a lost dog found its way to her house to fill Chochai's place. But when Parviz explained that the dog must have gotten lost or run away from an abusive owner, she looked at him questioningly. It happens, Parviz said—the little animal perked up her ears as if she understood exactly what he was saying—but in a safe and kind home Chochai would become herself again.

He gave Chochai a rabies shot and a heartworm pill and said he often felt that animals in the examining room knew that other animals had experienced pain there. Mrs. Yung give him a sad look. Oh my, she said, scratching Chochai's head.

Parviz asked Mrs. Yung to leave the dog for a few days so he could keep his eye on her and do some tests. Afternoons when Mrs. Yung came to check on the dog, they became better acquainted. When Chochai was released, he received the first of her invitations to supper.

At dinner the old couple seemed on edge and were particularly talkative, especially after a few glasses of the mijiu wine. Well, Mr. Yung said, sitting up in his wheelchair, another year has passed. Parviz could see how the old man's back looked more curved and his face more bony. Mr. Yung wiped his face with a crumpled handkerchief and repeated, Another year has passed, how amazing. Every year I think *that's it*, this is the year the earth will spin out of its orbit, but *no*, it keeps going. Parviz wanted to say he understood perfectly and had often thought that if the solar system didn't snap, one's mind might. Yes, Mr. Yung went on, another year has passed and here we are in the Year of the Dog. The dog days will go on. Let me tell you, Doctor, it was in the Year of the Dog that China was destroyed by those good-for-nothing people. Devastated by those who shouted, Let a hundred flowers bloom! He looked at Parviz as if he should know what he was talking about. Well, we'll see, he said again, we'll see what unseen things the year will bring. Time will tell.

Parviz smiled and remembered how the old man had murmured this same phrase the first time he met him. He'd asked where Parviz was from and if he'd ever thought of returning. It's too late for me, Mr. Yung went on, too late to go anywhere—if there were anywhere to go. Time will tell, he added. Time will tell.

Mrs. Yung patted the back of her husband's hand. My dear, she said, I think it was the Year of the Ox when the Communists came. She had told Parviz her husband was becoming more forgetful and often mixed things up. Sometimes he talked about when they got married in China and had their son, Taishi. We didn't get married in China, Doctor, it was in Honolulu, and this is where our son was born. She had no idea how he could forget that and thought it was the future her husband was afraid of and the more he dwelt on the past the more mixed-up his mind became. Sometimes he talked about the same thing or asked the same question for days.

I prefer the Year of the Pig, Mr. Yung said. Then he asked if Parviz knew that the pig was the twelfth animal to answer the Buddha's call to become domesticated. Parviz shook his head. Yes, he said, it was the pig. And then he had a coughing spell that made his whole body shake. After a moment, he caught his breath and went on. Doctor, you wouldn't believe the pigs we barbecued during the celebrations. In the days I fought alongside Chiang Kai-shek, any village we entered, the peasants would butcher pigs by the dozen for us.

Later in the kitchen, as they were drying the dishes and putting them away, Mrs. Yung said she didn't know where the stories about fighting with Chiang Kai-shek came from. Although of course it was true her husband had been in the military and hated the Communists.

What else goes on in the old man's head? Parviz wonders. Does he think of his only son, Taishi, whose picture is in the living room? In the picture, Taishi is standing in his pilot's uniform under the blade of a Cobra helicopter, his helmet under his arm and a clouded look in his eyes. Nearby is a portrait of the old man when he was very young, in the military uniform of the time, wearing high leather boots and carrying a sword, his eyes looking straight into the distance, impassive and penetrating.

Mr. Yung had encouraged Taishi to join the air force—had insisted, Mrs. Yung told Parviz—and urged him to go to Vietnam, believing that the Communists had to be defeated and not allowed to take over like they did in China. Six months later, Taishi's helicopter went down in the jungles of Vietnam. He was badly injured but survived, and after he was discharged moved to San Francisco and never came to visit. Mrs. Yung said she went and looked for him but thought he didn't stay in one place for long.

Parviz wonders whether Taishi hears his father's voice the way he hears his . . . Go—go away. Go be with your cats and dogs. A Muslim shouldn't touch a dog, and you become a dog doctor? I'm far away from you, Father, but not free of you, go ahead and aim your anger at me from the other side of the earth. In that antiquated world of yours, in that ancient desert city full of scorpions, be proud of your shop and your status in the old bazaar. Be proud and let your sources bring you confiscated goods from the houses of those who were executed or put in prison for their thoughts and beliefs or were lucky and ran out of the country with their lives. Here, far away from all of that and proud of my profession, I'll go on treating the sick cats and dogs and wouldn't change it for the world.

He looks around trying to clear his head and find a landmark or anything recognizable that would lead him home. Up the street he sees a narrow doorway. The top half of the plate glass door is covered with the image of a woman, her black hair spread out, her brow pinched, and her dark eyes narrow and piercing. At first he thinks it's an image of Pele. In her outstretched hands she's holding a black globe, and a deck of tarot cards is open in front of her. Arcing above her are the words, *Do you know where you are or where you're going? Don't be so sure!* He knows he's been around there before. Just a few blocks down the street is the Top of the Hill lounge where he used to go. What a surprise. How could he have not noticed this place? He tries to turn the doorknob. He'll come tomorrow, he tells himself, and consult with this unusual woman who is able to predict the future. Standing in the circle of yellow light coming from the lamp above the door, he put his face on the glass and peers into the narrow hallway, where an old wooden staircase goes up and vanishes in the darkness. I see you gypsy woman, he says softly, I see you in that old desert town. Hey, gypsy woman, it was you—didn't you once call out to me on my way home from school? Come over here, young man, you said. Under the spell of your Mesopotamian eyes, I moved closer. It was a cold winter afternoon and there was no energy left in the distant sun. You took my hand and held it between your warm palms. You'll journey far to find yourself, my friend, but you must be extremely careful—many have tried and many have been lost. And the worst way of being lost is being lost in your own mind. Be on a journey, but never be lost. You made sure I understood. Your whisper was a lullaby, it warmed my ears. I was certain you weren't from our mortal world, that you'd come to roam around and tease young men like me. Maybe you're here in the islands. I wish I could see you again and have you take my hand, read my palm, and look at me with those mesmerizing eyes. I remember the deck of cards you showed me. All the face cards with nude figures, and the joker—oh, what a devilish smile.

He steps back out of the circle of light, dazed. A woman in shabby clothes, with disheveled hair and a cigarette between her lips, passes by pushing a grocery cart. The wheels of the cart wobble and squeak. The cart is packed with old magazines and papers and things in plastic bags, some tied to the outside of the cart. What's inside them, God only knows. He hurries on and a block away sees a half dozen men standing in the parking lot of a church. One step at a time, brothers, one of them says to the others. The hunched-down man next to him reaches out and puts his hand on his shoulder. That's right, he says. Yes, brothers, Parviz says under his breath as he passes, good luck. Take it one day at a time. The climb is high and it's easy to fall.

He hasn't gone far when he hears a shuffling behind him. It seems close by. No, it's not the echo of his footsteps, he's sure of it. He thinks no one's there, but then notices an obscure figure, a shadow in the bushes. A man with long hair and beard is squatting on his haunches. He seems to be in his own world, a satisfactory smile on his face. He doesn't pay Parviz any attention. After a few steps, Parviz stops and looks back to see him stand up, pull up his pants, and tie the rope going through his belt loops. The man picks up his plastic bag and catches up with him, then takes out a small bottle from his pocket and holds it out. Realizing there's no sign of companionship, he shakes his head, takes a sip, and staggers away.

A car drives past, its tires plying the wet asphalt with a continuous whoosh. Parviz crosses Koko Head Avenue and walks by the open-air market, now closed. The smell of rotten tropical fruit follows him. He walks along the narrow street that slopes down the hill. The barking of dogs echoes in the valley. He's never heard so many. Look, Parviz—it's a voice from childhood days—look at all the dogs wandering the streets. Let's chase them away. See, I hit one. See how it whimpered and limped away? Throw the stone, Parviz. You're a sissy, Parviz.

He holds his head for a moment, then goes down the street, trying to keep his balance. It's silence he needs. Silence. He should go to the Buddhist temple where Mrs. Yung took him, if he can find it. It's light and quiet there. He'll go and sit in front of the Buddha Shakyamuni, he tells himself, the fat and happy Buddha with his centuries-old smile that receives everyone. There in light and silence the grand Buddha sits surrounded by hundreds of little Buddhas all in his image, all fat and happy, all smiling with heavenly calmness, filled with the ashes of the departed devotees who in days gone by sat in front of their beloved Buddha and are now in his care until the end of eternity. This time, if he ever goes there, he'll ask the monk for one of those little Buddhas for himself.

At the temple they sat in the lotus position in front of the Buddha almost all afternoon, their eyes closed and their hearts calm. Then they walked in the garden, breathing in the pungent tropical air. Mrs. Yung pointed out each orchid and asked which ones

Parviz liked the best. To his amusement, he was able to find something to say about their unique shapes and colors. She nodded approvingly. Oh, you like this one? That's the samurai orchid, Taishi's favorite. She said she used to bring Taishi there after he came back from Vietnam because it was one place he was able to relax. Afterward, Parviz promised himself he would go there anytime he needed silence, but he never did. He'll go tomorrow, he tells himself. That day in the garden, Mrs. Yung told him all about Taishi and what a wonderful boy he was when he was growing up, interested in everything and happy to go places with her. Then she asked Parviz about his childhood and his mother. He didn't say much, just the ordinary things, and ended up listening to her story of how it happened that she came to Hawai'i when she was only sixteen. She said that when she was a small girl in Manchuria, her family lived above her grandfather's teahouse. The store was always full of smoke and laughter and people telling stories. She didn't know at the time that they were smoking opium. Then the Communists came, overtaking the town, and soldiers, their swords drawn, made her grandfather and his friends kneel down in front of his shop. Her father hadn't let her see her grandfather's body. Soon after, he sold everything they owned so they could leave the country. He managed to put her and her mother on a ship bound for San Francisco, with the hope that he would make it out later, although he never did. Many people were running away, and Lee Yung was on the ship too. It was destiny, she said, that she met Lee, who was handsome and strong and kept the people on the boat from fighting and stealing. When they arrived in Honolulu, the captain made some excuse, saying that the boat couldn't make it all the way to San Francisco. Things had turned out well, though. There were jobs in the sugar cane and pineapple plantations, and a few years later she and Lee got married. Their son Taishi was a good boy, she said. Her husband had never recovered from his going away.

Parviz thought it was she who hadn't recovered, otherwise why the excess of interest in gardening and cuisines of the world and the shelves packed with cookbooks and books on gardening? He wonders about his own mother and how she was able to manage.

His trip back home after so many years was for her. He wanted to see her, to comfort her, but he couldn't find her. He knew she was there, though, he could feel it. She seemed close by, but he couldn't find her. Finally, Grandfather took him to her grave beside Grandmother's in the grove of dust-covered palm trees. Every night the wind laid down a layer of sand over the tombs and every morning his grandfather would kneel down and sweep away the sand with his old hands, murmuring, Az khak amadim, be khak bar migardim—we come from earth and return to earth.

Parviz feels feverish in the tropical night and his thoughts are fragmented. He kneels beside the bushes at the street corner, his head spinning and his heart in his throat. He hears the jingling of bells. Someone is there. A soft female voice rises. Hi there, whatcha doing? He turns and sees a pair of enormous clown boots and short baggy pants patched in different colors and, raising his eyes, takes in a skinny figure with a round red nose and red lips extended in an exaggerated grin, a bowler hat atop her head. A small poodle, its white fur droopy and wet, is at her heels. She stares down at him and points with a long finger, gesturing to get him to stand up. Her dog sniffs and circles around him. She likes you, she says in a childish voice. You must be all right if Muffin likes you. Want to come along on a journey with us? The circus is in Paradise.

She steps away, her dog following, then turns as if she wants to say something and suddenly bursts into laughter. Gotcha, she says. We're going to a kid's birthday party up the street. You can come along and be my assistant. You look perfect for the part. Can you juggle? He shakes his head. Can you sing? He shakes his head again. Surely you can sing—everybody can sing. You can hum along. *Come with me, come with me*, she sings softly, *come with me to the sea.* He struggles up and looks her way as she shuffles off with her dog, the little bells jingling at her ankle, and vanishes into the penumbra of palm leaves darkening the sidewalk.

Yes, that's what he'll do, he thinks, he'll go to the sea tomorrow. But tomorrow seems far away. For now he'll just keep on walking. There's peace in this drizzly night. But then comes the sudden cry of the high-surf sirens. He stops and looks around. The feel and smell of the ocean gets stronger and soon the rise and fall of the sirens dies out. It is several minutes before he starts off again. One weary foot following the other, he keeps on walking the dark streets. The skyline looks familiar and he knows he's no closer to home than when he started. He hears the jingling of tiny bells and thinks he's been drifting toward Magic Island all along.

DEPARTURES

It's been years, but by chance or fate there she is, sitting across from him at Logan airport in Boston. Her hair is short and lustrous, and her green eyes seem greener, with a few faint lines around them. She looks at him. He's sure she recognizes him, even though his once jet-black hair has gone totally gray.

"Do you remember?" he says.

"How could I forget?" Her eyes smile just the way he remembers. "And your accent! It still has its effect!"

He explains he's on his way from Honolulu to visit the old country after so many years. And she says she's going to Paris for the publication of her latest novel.

They walk through the terminal, stopping to browse in the shops. She is tall and slender, with a tranquility in her manner. At the bookstore, she flips through the bestsellers with an air of self-confidence that he remembers well. "I can't believe this book made it and that one won a prize. Look at this. A Pulitzer Prize—give me a break. Have you read it?" she asks.

He shakes his head. "No, I only read your novels."

"Oh, sure," she says, then picks out a magazine. "To get me through the flight."

They decide to have a drink at the airport bar. They order white wine and a cheese platter. "I miss Hawai'i," she says. "Sorry I never managed to come back for a visit."

"Right, you didn't."

"Maybe I will, who knows." She smiles. "Are you still working at the East-West Center?"

"Yes, still at it," he says.

"Still trying to bring the two worlds closer."

"I guess, no harm in trying."

"Tell me, do you still have your circle of friends? The yoga crowd from Silent Dance and your friends who went swimming at Magic Island?"

"Well, not so much. Not the way it used to be when you were around."

"How about your veterinarian friend—what was his name?—the introverted doctor who liked to talk about literature and wanted to be a writer. He saved my poor little dog Cashew. I was grateful."

"You mean Parviz. I don't see him very much. He keeps to himself more than ever."

She takes a drink of wine and looks at him intently, "Well I don't see any ring. My guess is you didn't marry the Afghan girl after all."

"No, I didn't," he says. "It was your imagination, or should I say your jealousy, that gave you that idea."

"No, not really. All the attention the family gave you, getting you to teach her and her brother English. Her beauty was out of this world, with that long black hair and those dark eyes, not shy but innocent." She smiles. "I was on the verge of falling in love with her myself. I was sure you'd eventually end up in an arranged marriage."

"Well, I didn't. And you left the Islands."

"I just had to," she says. "We went through all that, as I recall."

"Sure. And you, did you ever get married?"

"Are you kidding?" she says with a short laugh.

He's silent, looking at her and thinking how beautiful she still is. With her sharp eyes and round face and small nose, he always thought she looked like a delicate bird.

She leans toward him across the table. "Remember the doves?" she asks, a dreamy look in her eyes. "How they cooed in the early morning?"

176

"And the sprinklers?" he says. "The way they would go off, splashing the windows of the cottage and waking us up at dawn. Then we would make love and fall sleep again entangled until the tropical sun was high in the sky."

"Yes," she says softly. "I wonder if the cottage is still there in back of the big house."

Before he could answer yes, that it was still there and he'd often gone by and thought about the old days, her cell phone rings.

"Sorry, I have to take this—my publisher."

She moves toward the lobby where it is quieter, looking his way once in a while. He sees the cheerful expression on her face, reminding him she is as beautiful as the day they met years ago amid the flowering ginger that grows wild on the trail to Sacred Falls. The hike was long, always longer than people expected, and could be treacherous when it rained and the stream rose. That day, though, it was only wet and muddy. She had shared her chocolate bar with him and told him the story of Kamapua'a, the Hawai'ian demigod, half-pig half-man, and how he had made his home in the valley and lived there for hundreds of years until the day his enemies surrounded him and the only way out was the cliff at the far end of the valley. So Kamapua'a pressed his back against the cliff face, helping his family climb up to the top of the mountain and getting up the cliff to safety just as his enemies were about to close in on him. The waterfall is said to be the place where he pressed his back against the valley wall. She laughed and said she liked to think that the legend had it wrong, that it wasn't his family he helped to safety, but a secret lover.

She invited him to dinner at her cottage. They sat on the straw mats spread out on the floor. She had a white shirt on, and he loved how it was unbuttoned one button too low and notices she's still doing that. The night, the dinner, and the unbuttoned-one-button-too-low white shirt—he remembers it well. She had cut her finger opening a wine bottle and twisted a napkin around it to stop the bleeding. When he noticed a red spot on her white shirt, she saw him staring and suddenly pulled off her shirt and ran to the kitchen sink and held it under the tap. He followed and stood behind her, looking at the curve of her bare back. It was the first time he touched her.

The walls of her cottage were covered with island artifacts: wooden turtles and geckos and fishhooks carved from whalebone. He browsed the books on her small bookshelf—novels, collections of short stories, and books on Eastern painting and drawing—and pulled out a couple to ask her about. "That was the catch," she said later, "the spark that started the fire."

She told him about the stories she'd written, and later would read them to him on the warm tropical evenings. She liked to fan herself with the pages after they had exhausted themselves making love. In one story, a couple went for a moonlight swim on Lanikai Beach. She smiled mysteriously when he asked if he was the man in the story. He suggested she lighten up on the nude parts, but she said, "No way, that's what makes it exciting." He saw it in print a few years later with their intimacy described in detail.

She looks his way, smiles, and points to the phone, indicating she won't be long. He wonders what her latest book is about. For years he read everything she wrote, looking for his traces. The one she won a prize for—its title was *Ice*, although he would have named it *Fire*—he had a hard time reading. He knew that what had happened was just the opposite of what she had written, and that she wasn't the one who'd brought ice cubes to bed. It was clever how she turned it into a story of two lovers from a culture where people lived and died without having seen ice and how the chunk of ice they found deep in an ancient lava cave became an unforgettable part of their love-making and sent them on a search that lasted the rest of their lives.

He was in good shape then, young and cool-headed. He'd been kicked out of his homeland and by chance or fate had landed in "Paradise"—just the opposite of Adam, he would say—and dreamed of their staying there forever, cradled by the ebb and flow of the ocean. She had other dreams, though, and was stubborn in her way. She wanted to go to the East Coast and become the editor of a literary journal, and said that to succeed she needed to know another language and was learning French. "You can't stay in one place," she would say, "you have to go and see the world. The world won't come to you."

She glances his way, still talking, before finally putting the phone in her purse and coming back to the table. But they've barely started to talk when her flight is announced. She gets up and looks at him for a moment, then leans across the table and kisses him on the lips. When she straightens up, her green eyes are smiling again. He takes her hands in his. He doesn't want to let go, but can feel the anxiety of going in them. He lets go and sits down, the wine-glass curving cool and smooth in his hand as he watches her fade into the crowd.

DAY OF SOLITUDE

"The day belongs to us," she said. "A day just for me and you, away from the tourists." Arms linked, they walked across the cobblestone courtyard of the hostel Las Sombras.

"I'm glad we talked last night, even though we didn't get anywhere." She squeezed his arm.

"It was more like an argument," he said. "You kept repeating yourself."

"No more, okay? Let's enjoy our day away from this damp place."

"Okay, let's."

The old hostel, with its crenelated walls and Spanish arches, leaned against the mountainside as if trying not to slide downslope. When they reached the narrow archway leading to the cracked wooden gate, he slowed down, but with the tug of her arm walked on. If he stopped and listened, he thought he could hear the hooves of the conquistadores' horses echoing on the stones. He mentioned this to her the day they arrived at the hostel, but she had laughed, "Do you always have to imagine the strangest things?" she said. "Sounds from centuries ago!"

It was the second week of their South America trip, a belated honeymoon deferred for three years. They'd spent their first week at the seashore, swimming in the warm Pacific Ocean, eating seafood and drinking wine in the beachfront restaurants, and making love in their hotel room by the sea.

Here in this small mountain town, she wasn't yet used to the altitude and the frigid nights and he was getting impatient with her constant talk about their relationship and the "natural order of things," as she put it. He hadn't expected her to act this way, especially on this trip.

They walked down the steep alley toward the muffled sound of a brass band and found their way to the front of the crowd. There was a procession underway in the plaza. A long file of people crept past them, crosses and crucifixes bobbing above their heads. They found their way to the front of the crowd. A madonna and child borne on the shoulders of a dozen men wobbled from side to side with each step they took. The blood and tears on the cheeks of the statues seemed so real he felt he could reach out and wipe them away. It was as if an apparition from the past had, suddenly and unbidden, come alive before his eyes. The musicians in the brass band, all old and in blue uniforms that seemed too tight for them, played a mournful march as the women and girls swayed from side to side, their skirts swirly with colors. Behind them came a group of men and boys twisting wooden instruments that made a cracking sound, *krrrrrrrrr, krrrrrrrrr,* so loud he felt its vibration pass through his body.

He lost all sense of time. Beside him, his wife moved with the slow rhythm of the crowd. After a while she nudged him to indicate they should go.

The sun was high, and the gray stone buildings around the plaza had drawn back their shadows. They were halfway up the stairs in front of the cathedral when he suddenly stopped. He didn't want to face the shoeshine boys who had surrounded him the day before, insisting on shining his shoes, a chore he was fully capable of doing himself. He hated to have a barefoot boy kneeling down in front of him. With his eyes he pleaded with her to send the boys away, but she seemed to enjoy seeing him struggling with such a simple thing as saying, No, grácias, no necesito, and had only smiled. Later at the hostel she had teased him, calling him silly for the way he dealt with the boys and, when he looked at her seriously, kissing him and saying, "That's why I love you."

But today when they reached the top of the steps, no boys rushed over to them. He wondered whether they were somewhere in the crowd or were dancing or carrying crosses in the procession. Then he spotted four of them standing on their shoeshine boxes, trying to see over the heads of the crowd.

As the procession moved in the direction of the cathedral, the sound of the brass band reverberated more loudly. They watched for a few minutes before wandering toward the shade of the archways flanking the plaza, where rainbows of colored blankets were stacked up against the columns and they had to dodge the gloves and hats hanging down from the arches.

"Everything seems beautiful and simple here," she said.

"You think so?"

"Yes. I love it and hope it will always stay the same."

"You know it won't."

"Why not?"

"Because we're here."

"Well, it just might."

"Things change," he said. "People too. You, for example."

"What?" She stopped and narrowed her eyes. "Didn't we say we were going to have a good day?"

"That was the goal."

"It still is," she said. "What do you say we go and get something to eat? I'm hungry."

"In that case we'd better find a café before you faint from hunger—a simple café, one that hasn't changed." As soon as he said it, he wished he hadn't.

She looked at him again.

"Oh, come on," he said. "Don't take it to heart. I'm only joking."

"Don't joke."

"Sorry," he said and took her arm. They walked past the plateglass window of the Banco Comercial, the only modern building on the plaza. A woman in native dress sitting by a pile of handmade tablecloths held one out to them, smoothing the soft cloth, striped in reds and yellows, with rough fingers. "Mira—Señor, Señora," she pleaded in a soft voice.

They turned down a narrow street leading away from the plaza at an angle. The few people they encountered were hurrying in the opposite direction. He thought they might be going to the procession and was pleased they saw it. He wished they'd stayed longer, even though he avoided crowds and preferred to wander the empty old streets and shaded alleys of the city or visit ruins like the fortress they'd seen outside town two days earlier, where the walls, the air, the dust had all seemed familiar to him, as if he had been there before, had breathed the air and seen and heard the masons chiseling the massive stones and fitting them together with primitive tools and amazing craftsmanship.

A dog rooting in a pile of garbage looked at them nervously. In a side alley, a group of boys were playing soccer and shouting at one another as they chased an old plastic ball. The dust, the heat, and the excitement of the boys made him think of the days he played soccer, exactly like these boys, in the alley and then, years later as a student at UC Davis, when he and Parviz would play with a group of friends. Parviz had studied to be a veterinarian and moved to Hawai'i. He never visited Parviz as he promised he would. He wondered if they should have gone to Hawai'i instead of coming here, but then he would have missed everything he'd seen. She pulled on his sleeve and he started to walk again. Farther down the street a sign came into view—Café de Solitude. Outside, a young girl sat on the sidewalk with a guitar on her lap and a tarnished copper bowl in front of her. When she saw them, she started to play, her tiny voice accompanying the low sound of the strings.

"What a sweet girl. Why don't you give her some change?"

He searched his pockets. When he bent down and dropped in the coins, the bowl rang with a dull metallic sound. Taking his eyes away from the girl, he straightened up and hesitated for a moment before walking on, in spite of wanting to hear the happy-sounding song to the end.

The café was open to the street and sunlight stretching into the room illuminated a wall covered with azure tiles and painted scenes of llamas and Andean people on green mountainsides. All the tables were empty except one close to the entrance, where a young couple with a little girl were sitting.

They chose a table on the shaded side of the room. He sat opposite her, facing the street. A waiter brought the menus. "Buenas tardes. A su servicio."

They ordered beer and watched the little girl in her white Sunday dress sitting beside her mother eating.

"Look how pretty she is," she said.

"Yes," he said, turning.

"What are you thinking about?" she asked after a moment.

"Nothing in particular," he said, looking at her pale blue eyes and remembering how beautiful she looked with her skin picking up a tan, how lovely she was when she was calm, and how dearly he loved her. He wondered how they could keep things from taking a bad turn and whether he would be able to come to terms with the "natural order of things" that she kept talking about. In the past, she had said things like this only in passing, but now she was speaking more openly. He thought they'd been in agreement when they got married, and now he was realizing that she had changed her mind and was serious about it.

He felt thirsty and was glad when the waiter came and filled their glasses with one smooth movement. A boy was standing at the front of the café, his eyes moving back and forth between the waiter and the little girl, who was playing at feeding a chicken bone to her doll. He noticed the boy's shirt with all its buttons missing and wondered if he had been one of the boys playing soccer.

They ordered huevos con papas fritas and frijoles negros. The waiter, noticing the boy, went to the front of the café and shooed him away. The boy moved to the other side of the street but, as soon as the waiter returned to the kitchen, came back to the same spot, his eyes watchful.

"I've been thinking," she said. "Why don't we go back to the coast for the rest of our trip? I liked it better there. The altitude is making me dizzy and it's cold at night. Besides, there aren't any good restaurants and no seafood—just papas, huevos, and frijoles. And the hostel—hot water for only an hour in the morning."

185

He tried to listen, but his attention was on the boy, who disappeared again when the waiter came back with their food. The waiter put the plates down and took a glass of milk to the little girl.

"How about it, can we go back?"

"What?" he said.

"You weren't listening, were you?"

"Yes I was," he said. "What did you say?" He raised the steaming food to his mouth and saw the boy again on the same spot, looking at him. When their eyes met, he put his fork down.

"Why aren't you eating?" she said. "It's not bad."

He took another bite, but the peppery taste of the beans made his stomach turn.

"I was saying we've seen enough here."

"Don't be so sure," he said.

"Well, what else is there to see in this little town?"

He didn't answer and turned his eyes to the family, who were getting ready to leave. The man counted out a few bills and put them on the table. As soon as they stepped out of the restaurant, the boy leaped toward the table, grabbed as many as chicken bones as he could, and vanished down the street.

"What was that?" she asked, turning to look.

"Didn't you see? That boy . . ." He fell silent.

She watched him staring into the distance. "I can't understand how you suddenly sink into a lost state and forget I'm sitting across from you."

He heard her voice, but the scene with the boy was repeating itself before his eyes—a hundred times, a thousand times, as fast as photons could travel—going farther and farther into his memory, somewhere beyond his power to control, to a place set aside for things like this to sink in and remain alive. After a moment, he looked at her and then back at the table. Water was dripping from a tipped-over glass.

"You didn't see . . ." He became silent, thinking that she didn't need to know, that he had seen it and that was enough. "I'm sorry," he said, reaching for her hand. "What were you saying?"

"Never mind," she said. "Let's eat." Then, seeing him staring at his plate, she pushed hers away. "Here's what I wanted to say. I can't understand why you don't see how flustered you make me. Take the shoeshine boys or the girl singing in the street or even the boy outside the café who you think I didn't see. You know, these things affect me too, but the difference is that I don't get so emotional that I forget myself. Didn't we come here to experience another culture? Otherwise we could have just stayed home and read books about it." She hesitated. "I have thoughts and desires, too, you know."

"Yes," he said after a while, "I know about your desires. It's all I've been hearing about. Desires change, but principles shouldn't change. I thought we understood that. I thought we had agreed on one important thing."

"Yes, you may be right," she said softly, "but we all change, we all go through transformations one way or another, hopefully for the better. And to be honest, I'm not happy hearing the same things from you either."

"What things?"

"About how the world is unjust and unsafe and we shouldn't condemn another soul to it." She waited, her eyes moist. "But that's enough for now, we don't need to talk about it now. All I wanted was to be together and have a pleasant day, and now half the day is gone."

Church bells rang out from somewhere close by. He looked toward the street. It seemed brighter and warmer, and a scrim of dust was rising from the cobblestones. He didn't want to leave. The sun would be blinding and heavy on his head and shoulders. She would be leaning on his arm, there would be more talk of the natural order of things, and he would have to debate with himself whether he could come to terms with it. But they had to go, because the afternoon was here, and soon the night, and then tomorrow, another day on the way.